HER DIRTY RANCHERS

A MEN AT WORK REVERSE HAREM ROMANCE

MIKA LANE

HEADLANDS PUBLISHING

COPYRIGHT

SHOP
Mika Lane

1

RUBY WHITAKER

"Oh my god, Mary. It's so, so good to see you."

She stared at me like she'd seen a ghost.

Awkward.

It was okay, though. I hadn't been back in a long time. She probably needed a moment to recognize me. I looked different now. Hell, I *was* different now. The big city will do that to you.

In my years away, I'd changed just about every aspect of myself that I could. Not that there was anything wrong with where I was from or who I used to be. I'd just wanted to leave everything about being from a ranch behind.

Like, really, really far behind.

"Mary, it's me, *Ruby*," I said to her still-blank face.

Mary, herself, was little changed. Her long black hair was newly scattered with tinsel-y silver, and her skin revealed a few lines that gave her a striking maturity. That was it. And even if the changes *had* been dramatic, I would have recognized her stout figure in the apron she'd worn for the twenty-plus years she'd served as my parents' cook and general housekeeper.

"Ruby Lee," she whispered, as if the words tasted strange in her mouth.

My stomach dropped. Mary was usually thrilled to see me come home. All my life, she'd not only been a member of my parents' household staff, but also my default babysitter-slash-nanny while my parents were busy growing their ranch business. There'd been times when my brother and I had seen more of Mary than our mom and dad together.

Which had been fine. Even preferable. She spoiled us rotten.

Which made it even more strange that she was looking at me like she had no fucking idea what I was doing here.

"Mary, are you okay?"

I stepped over the threshold into the house. She didn't step aside to let me enter, which put us in an awkwardly close proximity.

If I didn't know better, I'd think she was trying to block me from entering my own house.

"Um..." she stammered, continuing to stand her ground.

Oh my god. Had she had a stroke and no one told me? Or early-onset dementia?

I reached out, putting a hand on her arm. "Mary. It's me, Ruby. The Whitakers' daughter."

That would jog her memory. Or jog something.

Her head twitched, and she blinked, clearing her throat. "Sorry, honey. I am just so surprised to see you. Here. At the ranch."

Ohthankgod.

She was fine.

I stepped farther into the house, brushing against her since she still hadn't made way for me to enter.

I wondered where my parents were. It was getting to be dinner time.

Now that I was fully in the foyer, I took a deep inhale, and the house, as it always had, smelled of cedar, pine, and something delicious cooking in the kitchen. I'd been driving for more than ten hours and was freaking starved, having eaten only Clif bars and Red Vines. From all the sugar, I felt like I had hair on my teeth.

I did a full three-sixty in my parents' giant foyer, taking in the massive central staircase, exposed ceiling beams, and hunting trophies covering the walls. Nothing had changed, not even a little bit.

And I was thrilled.

I turned back to Mary, who, this time, put a hand on *my* arm.

"Honey. Can you wait here for just a second?"

Huh? Wait? In my own house?

But I didn't want to be pushy. Or get off on the wrong

foot. After all, it had been a while since I'd been around the ranch. I didn't want to act like a brash New Yorker.

"Sure, Mary."

She hustled off in the direction of my dad's office, and while I waited I bounced up and down a little in my sneakers. I'd always wanted to surprise my parents by coming home unannounced.

They were going to be so thrilled to see me. I'd pictured their reaction during the whole cross-country drive.

I could see it now.

Mom would cry when she saw me.

Dad would shake his head and laugh. Maybe get a little choked up, but clear his throat really fast the way guys did.

They'd want to know what brought me home, how long I'd be staying, and whether or not I was hungry.

Some of their questions I'd put off answering. Like why the hell I was there.

I'd tell them later that I *had* to come back to Flood Creek. Because I *had* to leave New York. Later.

They'd throw their arms around me and squeeze until I couldn't breathe. When they finally let go, Mom would offer me something to eat and Dad would go out to the car to get my stuff. We'd have an amazing dinner with yummy wine, thanks to Mary, and then we'd either watch a movie or play cards until we couldn't keep our eyes open any longer.

I'd wake the next morning with the sun streaming in

my bedroom, coffee brewing and bacon sizzling downstairs in the kitchen, where I'd wander wearing my flannel PJs and shearling slippers.

Like a real rancher's daughter.

At least that's what I pictured, until I realized the joke was on me. And it was a big, fat, fucking not-funny joke.

While waiting for whatever was taking Mary so freaking long to allow me into my own house, I wandered over to the credenza where my parents' incoming mail was always kept.

Odd. It was empty. Not a newspaper or ranching magazine in sight.

And where were my mom's usual vases of flowers?

They'd probably changed up their system, with the internet delivering everything digitally these days.

But still. My parents and the internet didn't mix much. At least not that I was aware of.

"Um, Ruby Lee?" Mary asked from behind me.

My smile blazing, I whipped around, prepared to run into the arms of one or both of my parents.

Instead, my stomach dropped.

Standing before me with an expression that could best be described as *what the fuck*, was Roman Maxwell.

Our neighbor from the next ranch over.

I hadn't seen him since I last babysat for his kids, long before I'd even left Flood Creek for college. He was still the handsome outdoorsman I remembered, with a splash more gray around the temples and deeper lines etched in his face.

And he was tall. So freaking tall.

Why was Roman Maxwell, who also happened to be my dad's biggest enemy, in our house?

2

RUBY

"Mr. Maxwell…?" My voice came out like a strangled squeak, and I swallowed hard. I needed water.

"Ruby Lee," he said, "could you come with me, please?"

He gestured in the direction of my father's office.

Because I was so thoroughly thrown off by seeing him, I mutely followed, with Mary patting me on the back, entering the room where I used to do homework while my father read the paper.

"Have a seat," he said, making himself at home behind my father's desk.

Where were the family photos and other mementos my dad kept on display? The place had been wiped clean.

But I spied the needlepoint pillow I'd made in 4-H on the crackled leather sofa between the bookcases. At least that was still there.

Dad would not be happy to know Roman Maxwell was behind his desk. But I wasn't saying anything until I had a better idea of what the hell was going on.

Mary lingered in the doorway. I waved her in and pulled out the chair next to me so she'd take a seat. Having her close by was a comfort.

I really wanted to hold her hand, but I wasn't ten years old.

After waiting for me to stop looking around and focus, Mr. Maxwell leaned his elbows on my father's desk and wove his fingers together. "I'm surprised to see you, Ruby Lee."

No shit.

"I go by *Ruby* now. Not Ruby Lee." I wasn't sure what else to say.

I glanced in Mary's direction, and she smiled kindly.

Awkward silence.

"I take it you haven't been in touch with your parents?" he asked.

What business was that of his?

He must have seen the scowl on my face, because he didn't wait for me to respond. "Ruby Lee, I'll get right to the point since it seems you need to be brought up to speed. I'm sorry I'm the one who has to tell you, because I'm sure it will come as a surprise. But the fact is, your parents sold Flood Creek Ranch to me. Several months ago, in fact. They sold me this house with most everything in it. They sold me all the animals and outbuildings. They even let me hire Mary here. They packed up and left the state, last I heard."

Was this a joke? Were my parents going to jump out at any minute and scream *surprise*? Because it wasn't fucking funny.

It was impossible. My parents would never sell to anyone, much less Roman Maxwell, who my dad hated with a passion.

And they wouldn't skip town without telling *me*. For Christ's sake.

I waited, looking around, wondering where they might pop out from, and imagining their surprise. But there was no popping. No surprising.

"Mary. Is this true?"

She grimaced, and after a moment slowly nodded. "Yes. They've left and they sold everything, sweetie. Even the furniture," she said, gesturing around.

Even the fucking pillow I'd needlepointed for them. As a gift.

"*You're* still here," I said.

"Mr. Maxwell was nice enough to keep me on."

He sat back in his chair and smiled. I had to say he was quite the silver fox even though I wanted to throw the ugly paperweight on his desk at him, which my brother had made for dad one Father's Day. Apparently, Mr. Maxwell was now the owner of that family treasure, as well.

He chuckled. "It was more like I begged her to stay, rather than *kept her on*."

Neither of them was making sense. I gripped my armchair and the room began to move around me.

"Mary, could you get Ruby Lee some water?" Mr. Maxwell asked.

She brought her hand up to my cheek. "Oh my. You're clammy, Ruby Lee. Hang on just a moment."

Water would be good. While I waited, I just stared at my feet and took deep breaths.

"I'm sorry you had to find out this way, Ruby Lee."

I realized I might never get anyone in Flood Creek to call me *Ruby*.

I was sure he could see the wreckage in my eyes. Although, I wasn't sure exactly who I was wrecked by— Mr. Maxwell, my parents, or myself for not knowing a goddamn thing about what was going on in my child-hood home.

I gulped the water Mary returned with and I was momentarily calmed. "I don't... I don't know why... my parents... didn't say anything to me." Shit. Now I was getting choked up.

My father hated Maxwell, and I was sure Maxwell hated him back. And now he probably thought his enemy's daughter was a pathetic loser.

"Mr. Maxwell, what about your ranch?" I asked.

He sat back in my father's chair, raking his hands through his thick hair. "I kept my ranch. I consolidated the two."

Well. Goody for him.

I pushed myself to my feet. Mary hovered to make sure I didn't fall over.

"I... I'm going to step outside for a moment to call my parents."

Maxwell nodded, and Mary looked at me with sympathy.

I hated when people felt sorry for me.

As I headed for the front door, I grabbed the purse and duffel I'd dropped in the foyer not ten minutes before, when I really thought I was *home*, because if what Maxwell told me was true, I couldn't leave my crap all over the place.

"Mom?" I snapped the second she'd answered her cell.

"Ruby Lee, honey! Good to hear your voice." In the background, she told my dad I was on the phone.

"Hey, Ruby Lee," Dad said when she put me on speaker.

"Um, where are you guys?" I asked.

Silence.

"Oh. Well, we're... driving," Mom stammered after a moment's hesitation.

"Okay. But where, Mom?" I demanded.

She changed the subject. Or tried to. "Hey, your father and I have a surprise for you," she said in a singsong voice.

It was nice that somebody was happy.

"Mom, I asked where you were."

More silence.

"Well, where are *you*, Ruby Lee?" Dad asked.

I was so not enjoying this.

"I asked you guys first."

Mom sighed. "We're out for a drive. No big deal. What's this interrogation all about, Ruby Lee?"

"Let me tell you, Mom. I'm at the ranch. Flood Creek Ranch. You remember that place? Your home. My home? Our home?"

She gasped and I could hear my father swearing under his breath like he did.

"Honey, how… how can you be at the ranch?"

"Easy, Mom. I drove here in a rental car. From New York. So I'm here. Right now. Sitting on the front steps. Looking over the valley. Which is lovely, by the way."

I could see them looking at each other in a panic. Dad would probably pull over at the next rest stop so they could compose themselves.

"Well now, honey, your father and I are on our way to New York City to see *you* in our new RV. It was supposed to be a surprise."

Un-fucking-believable.

Where to start?

I tried to calm my voice, but the truth was, I was inches from losing it. "You might have told me, Mom. *Because I'm not there*. Meaning you will get to New York, and not see *me*, because I'm in Montana to see *you*."

"Shit," she said.

In the background they bickered in muffled voices.

But I wasn't done. "Mom, I just saw Roman Maxwell, who tells me everything here is his now because he bought it. What the hell is going on?" I asked shrilly, getting louder with each word.

"Oh, honey. We were going to tell you when we got to New York. Well, I guess we don't have to continue there, now. Although your father and I really do enjoy a few days in the Big Apple..."

"Mom. Focus. Why is Mr. Maxwell telling me he owns the ranch now?"

Mom took a deep breath. "Because he does. Your father and I cashed out. Sold everything. We bought an RV and are traveling around the country now. Seeing all the sights."

I rubbed at a chip on my parents' front steps, the result of a long-ago fight with my brother over a toy dump truck. Mr. Maxwell's front steps, now.

"Traveling the country? I don't get it."

"Neither you nor your brother wanted to take over the ranch, and it was time for us to retire. Roman Maxwell offered us a very good price. We're living the RV lifestyle now. We plan to hit as many campgrounds as we can and really see the country. There are so many places we haven't been, the ranch always kept us so busy..."

She rambled on about the adventures they'd have and the new friends they'd make while the grass lawn in front of me heaved in rhythm with my stomach.

"Mom, when are you guys coming back? Now that you don't have to go all the way to New York, can you come back to Montana?"

"Oh no, honey. We're on the road. We won't be back in Montana for a very long time."

Great. Just fucking great.

"Mom, I wish you'd told me."

"We were going to, as soon as we got to New York."

Instead, they surprised me from wherever they were in the sprawling United States, and I was stuck in Flood Creek, with nowhere to go.

Living the RV lifestyle, my ass.

3

ROMAN MAXWELL

"I ALWAYS KNEW THAT WHIT WHITAKER WAS AN ASSHOLE. Now he's proved it again."

Mary gave me her best stink eye. Couldn't blame her. She'd worked for the Whitakers twenty-plus years. I'd hope she'd have some loyalty toward them.

But still.

"Mary, they freaking sold the ranch, took off, and neglected to tell their daughter? In what universe is something like that okay?"

She clicked her tongue like she did when she didn't approve. The woman had been working for me for only a couple months, but it hadn't taken long to learn her ticks and understand that while she might be household staff, she didn't hold back her opinions.

I'd had mad respect for her since day one. I couldn't deny it. I'd be lost without her.

"Roman, I'm sure there's a good explanation. The Whitakers don't operate irresponsibly."

Hmmm. I had some thoughts about how they operated, but kept them to myself.

"I hope not."

Because the look on that kid's face nearly tore my guts out.

Although, she wasn't much of a kid any longer.

When was the last time I'd seen her? Must have been when she was babysitting my kids, just before her father and I had fallen into the feud of the century. Never saw her again after that. She wasn't allowed over, which was too bad because the kids loved her. I didn't blame her, though. It was how her petty father operated.

Shit, that all had happened fifteen years ago. Seemed like a lifetime. Ruby Lee must have been thirteen or fourteen at the time, which would put her at twenty-eight, twenty-nine, now. From our quick meeting a minute ago, she was a far cry from the chubby, frizzy-haired kid she used to be. I'd heard she'd gone off to New York or someplace like that, and I had to say it looked good on her. She'd slimmed down with curves in all the right places, and she had a short, sleek haircut, the kind you didn't really see much around places like Flood Creek.

I didn't know about Ruby Lee, but the years had passed quickly for me. My kids had mostly grown, the wife had left me, and while the feud was never resolved, Whitaker sold me everything he had like he couldn't get out of town fast enough. His kids weren't interested in taking over the ranch, he'd told me via mail—he couldn't bring himself to speak to me face-to-face—and he and the wife wanted to retire. Apparently, I offered him the right price. His attorney sent me papers the next day and the deal was set in motion. He cashed out and said so long to Flood Creek. Wouldn't be surprised if he never stepped foot in the town again.

With Mary sitting right there in front of me, I casually walked over to the window facing the front of the house, peering out like I was assessing the day's weather. But what I was really doing was checking out Ruby Lee. I'd only gotten a quick eyeful of her and the single guy in me wanted more.

What could I say? Desirable women in Flood Creek were few and far between. And I hadn't been with a female in far too long.

I watched her sitting on my front steps, her head in her hands.

I had no doubt she was hurting, and I felt for her.

She looked small and vulnerable as she lifted her head off her knees and scanned the horizon of the ranch where she'd grown up. She was a lucky kid to have had free run of her father's ten thousand-plus acres, where she could do as she pleased without getting into any serious trouble.

It was the life my ex and I had wanted for our kids. And which, in the end, I suppose drove us apart.

Ruby Lee stood from the front step and dusted herself off. She wiped under her eyes and put her hands on her hips, looking around like it was the last time she'd see the place.

Then she turned and rang the doorbell.

I looked to Mary. "Shit. This is terrible. But there's nothing I can do about it. Is there?"

Mary's chin lifted as she stood to answer the door. "There most certainly is something you can do to help her. She grew up here, Roman. You can't just cast her out. She's a Whitaker."

Shit. I hadn't planned for a long-absent daughter to be part of the Flood Creek Ranch deal.

When I thought back, my beef with Whit Whitaker could have been resolved without too much trouble. He owed me money for letting his cattle graze on my land. It had been my naïve mistake to settle for a verbal agreement, rather than something written. When it came time for him to pay… crickets. He'd never intended to give me a damn cent. I had my attorney contact him and learned that because I had nothing in writing, I was shit out of luck.

I knew I could round up his cattle on my land and hold them for payment, but I didn't want to get involved in a shit show like that. I built a fence on the border of our property, and that was the end of that.

But I'd never trusted the fucker again, and he knew it. I'd made sure all the other ranchers at the local livestock council knew how he operated, and his reputation went down the shitter. That hurt him far more than the few thousand bucks he'd owed me.

I was glad to do it.

4

—————

ROMAN

MARY BROUGHT RUBY LEE BACK INTO MY OFFICE WHERE
she stood wringing her hands.

"I just want to say I'm sorry I barged in like this. I had
no idea. My parents hadn't told me because they were
heading to New York to surprise me, while I was heading
here to surprise them." She looked down and shook her
head sadly. "I feel so stupid."

From the corner of my office, Mary was side-eyeing
me. I knew what I had to do.

Ruby Lee sniffled and held her head back up, like she
was trying to be brave. "I'll get out of your hair now."

Mary walked over and put a hand on her arm, glow-
ering at me. "Wait a minute, honey. Where are you
going?"

21

She took a deep breath. "I'll go to the hotel in town."

Mary shot me a look.

Well, damn. "Um, Ruby Lee, the hotel burned down a couple years ago. It hasn't been rebuilt. Permitting issues."

I don't know what shocked her more, knowing her childhood home was sold off or that the Flood Creek hotel was gone. Because that's when she sank into the chair opposite my desk and covered her face with her hands.

"Shit, shit, shit," she murmured. "What about the saloon? Did the Flood Creek Saloon burn too?"

It was funny to see my former babysitter so concerned about the saloon. But she was plenty old enough to enter one, that was for sure.

I gave a small laugh. I couldn't help it. "Yes. The saloon is still there."

She actually looked a little relieved, probably more for the comfort of something familiar than an actual place to drink and hang out with ranch hands and cowboys.

"In spite of my differences with your father, I'd like to invite you to stay here for a bit. You know, until you figure out a plan. The house is huge, and your old room is probably exactly how you left it."

Despite her father's shortcomings, she'd been good to my kids for the period of time she'd been their babysitter.

And I tried not to go through life being *too* big of an asshole. If I could help her, I would.

A huge smile crossed Mary's face, and Ruby Lee's eyes opened wide.

"What about your kids? And Mrs. Maxwell?"

Oh boy. I'd known that was coming.

"Mrs. Maxwell and I split a while back. The kids are with her."

Those words still stuck in my throat. I supposed they always would.

"Oh. I'm so sorry."

Yeah. Everyone was sorry. Except for my ex-wife.

"How are the kids? I guess they're teenagers now?" she asked.

I started walking toward my office door, eager to wrap up any conversation about my family.

"Don't see much of them. They're still angry with me over the divorce."

Even though it was their mother's idea to split up.

"C'mon. Let's get your stuff out of the car."

I led them to the foyer, where Ruby Lee stopped. "I don't know, Mr. Maxwell. I… I'm not sure my parents would be comfortable with this."

"It's no problem. And I wouldn't worry about your parents right now. If it weren't for them, you wouldn't be in this situation."

As I got closer to Ruby Lee's car, I realized it was completely packed. Like *you can't see out the windows* packed. Why would someone bring so much stuff just for a visit?

"Ruby Lee, are you here for a short stay? Or something longer?"

I knew I shouldn't pry. I'd already taken on more than I was comfortable with by offering her a place to stay. But this was not the luggage of someone coming home for a week or two. This was what your car looked like when you'd moved out of someplace.

She avoided my gaze by leaning into the car to start pulling out suitcases, duffel bags, and even large green trash bags stretching at their seams.

"Visiting, Mr. Maxwell." She gave me a quick smile, and with loaded arms, we headed up to her old room.

Mary led the way, with me following Ruby Lee. And I had to say, her snug jeans looked damn good.

Jesus. I was ogling the babysitter. Although she hadn't been a babysitter in fifteen years.

So was I an old perv or not?

Ruby Lee dropped everything on the floor of her room and looked around marveling. "Oh my god, it's exactly the same."

She walked over to her small desk and opened the top drawer. "Cripes, my 4-H ribbons are still here."

I dropped my armload on her bed and headed down for another.

"Let me get the last of my stuff, Mr. Maxwell," she called, running after me. "I can't let you do it."

"Ruby Lee, please call me Roman. Mr. Maxwell sounds old. Very old."

She smiled at me, the first time I'd seen her do so since she'd arrived. "Okay. Roman. And please call me Ruby. I dropped the Lee part a long time ago."

I could see that. Ruby suited her much better.

"Guess you didn't want that country girl name anymore?" I asked.

She hesitated. I was pretty sure she didn't want to offend me.

"Go ahead. You can say it," I said as she piled my arms with the rest of the crap from her car.

"It's a country name for sure, Mr. Maxwell—I mean Roman. I dropped it the moment I left town. The only people who call me that are here in Flood Creek."

On our second trip, I led the way up the stairs to force myself to stop staring at her ass, and just as we neared the top, one of Ruby's duffel bags blew out, exploding clothing all over, followed by a curling iron that went clattering down the stairs.

"Oh, no." She stopped to gather her things.

I dropped off my armful of stuff in her room, where Mary was organizing, and came back to help with the mess. I walked to the bottom of the stairs to grab the appliance that had come out of her bag when she hollered after me.

"I've got that Roman. Let me get it," she said, running toward me with her arm outstretched.

"That's okay, Ruby, I got it—"

Oh. Shit.

It wasn't a curling iron that had tumbled down the stairs. Or any other sort of hair appliance.

Ruby's face turned bright red when I turned a giant vibrator over to her.

"Thank you," she said, pulling her shoulders back and marching right back up the stairs. In her free hand, she grabbed an armful of clothes and kept walking toward her room.

And I was trying like hell not to laugh.

Well, fuck me.

5

Ruby

"Thank you for all the help. And the place to stay. I... I really appreciate it."

It was weird to thank someone for letting me stay in a home that was mine, or at least used to be.

I still couldn't believe my parents had fucking sold.

Roman and Mary left me, pulling my door closed, and I stood staring at the vibrator in my hand. It had been a goodbye gift from my girlfriends in New York, a sort-of joke because I was the last one in the group to have anything like a vibrator, and because my leaving town was the perfect reason to pony up for an expensive gift. I might have preferred a new handbag or some such, but I kept that to myself.

And now Roman and Mary had seen it before I'd even tried the damn thing out.

I plopped down on the edge of my bed—a double I'd moved over from my brother Bud's room when he'd left home years ago. Although it really wasn't my bed anymore. It was Roman Maxwell's now.

How do you just sell something that is living and breathing, full of laughter and fights, and the sorts of trials every family goes through? Did my parents realize what they'd done? It was like they'd killed something precious.

The ranch was the soul of our family. It was just… disrespectful. That's what it was, disrespectful of the ranch. And our family.

How did they just trade it for cash? And to someone my father claimed to have hated for half my life.

I knew little about what had gone down between my dad and Roman way back when. At the time, when I'd asked why I couldn't babysit the Maxwell kids any longer, my mother had said *don't worry about it*, like she always did when a subject was not open for discussion.

But babysitting wasn't the only way I was impacted by what had happened between the two men. Mr. Maxwell had previously taken my brother, me, and some of the other 4-H'ers out on the occasional horseback riding expedition. They had been nothing less than magical, as I remembered.

We'd ride for a while, take a break by having lunch and a swim in the creek, and ride back home. I'd thought I was in heaven. Mr. Maxwell had been so kind and patient, especially with me, who'd not been completely comfortable on horses since a spill I had when I was younger. Sure, kids on a ranch have the opportunity to do things like that all the time, but how often did an adult take the time to treat you like you were a normal person and not just a dumb kid?

We'd had a few expeditions like that, and then they came to a screeching halt. Bud and I had tried to figure out what was going on, and got some information from a kid at school whose dad was also a rancher.

Something about someone owing the other guy money.

To our adolescent minds, it seemed silly. If someone owed money, why didn't they just pay? But we were too young to understand the nuances of business agreements and the egos of alpha men. All we knew was that riding with Mr. Maxwell was over, and my babysitting jobs were too. We'd hoped our own dad would take up the slack. When we initially asked him, he was interested. Excited, even. But when it came down to it, he never had the time.

After that, Dad spoke about Mr. Maxwell as if he were the devil incarnate. Naturally, I'd assumed everything he said was fact. Why would I think otherwise?

He was a bad man, and I was never to go near his house or children again.

So, Mr. Maxwell's—I mean Roman's—offer to let me crash was a mind-blowingly kind gesture. Of course, if he hadn't offered, I would have just hidden my car behind the old barn and sneaked into one of the bunkhouses like I did when I was a kid, and leave the next morning before he'd noticed.

Having my old room sure beat the hell out of that option.

I looked around, marveling how everything in my room was exactly as I'd left it. It was cool and creepy at the same time. I was happy—actually, thrilled—for something familiar and comfortable, but it was also like entering a time capsule filled with my old high school bedspread, pennants from all the colleges I'd applied to, and even my old Avon perfume bottles.

All sold to Roman Maxwell. How fucked was that?

My mother was famous for never throwing anything out. Which made it all the more strange that she and my dad had packed up and left. How does someone who's a borderline hoarder walk away from all their shit?

There was a soft knock on my door. "Ruby Lee," Mary called quietly.

I shoved the vibrator, which for some reason I was still holding, under my bed. "Come on in."

She poked her head through a crack in the door. "Hey, honey. I wanted to bring you some clean sheets, and also a sandwich in case you're hungry before I head home."

Well, shit. Now my eyes were filling again.

"Thank you, Mary," I said in a cracking voice.

What a freaking godsend she was.

She took a seat next to me, the bed creaking. It had never been a very good bed, my brother having taken it off a friend's hands, but I'd been thrilled at the time to graduate from my childish twin. In fact, I was so excited it probably wouldn't have mattered if it had freaking bed bugs.

"Guess you've had quite the day, huh?" she said.

I'd forgotten how starving I'd been until I took a bite of the sandwich.

I nodded. "Crazy stuff, Mary. But how lucky am I that you're still here? And look at my room, with everything still intact. It's really nice of Mr. Maxwell—I mean, Roman—to let me crash. Although I can't freaking believe my parents sold this all to him."

She stood to go. "Your parents thought you didn't want it. You'd been gone so long. And Roman is a good man, Ruby Lee. He'd never turn you out."

I winced. "*Ruby*. Please," I reminded her.

She fake-smacked her forehead. "Ruby. It may take me a couple tries to get it. Don't hesitate to remind me if I slip."

I jumped up to hug her. "Thank you, Mary. Thank you for everything. I'm so happy you're still here. I don't know what would have happened if you hadn't been."

"You're welcome, sweetie. Get some sleep. I'll be back in the morning. And try not to blow a fuse with that damn... electric thing of yours."

She laughed all the way down the stairs.

NEXT DAY, I drove the few miles to town to see how much the place had changed, and whether if I might find a little apartment or cottage for rent.

Roman hadn't been kidding about the hotel having burned. I pulled my car over on the opposite side of the street to take a good look and found that all that was left was the brick façade and remnants of the fireplace that had lent the creaky old place some charm. It had been a cool building, definitely old school and quirky, and according to some, haunted.

And just as Roman had said, the Flood Creek Saloon, right next door, was unscathed. It looked just as dumpy as it ever had, but bore no signs of having been touched by the fire.

It was a miracle, that one old wooden building would burn and the one next to it remain intact.

I kept driving until I reached the grocery store, which I knew had apartments above it.

"Do you know who rents the places upstairs?" I asked a gum-snapping woman at the check out.

She pushed her shaggy mullet behind her ears and pointed to herself. "Yup. I do. You want to see the one I have vacant?"

Hope surged through me, and it felt damn good considering the devastation of finding out my parents had bailed on the ranch.

"Do you have short term leases?" I asked.

She looked me up and down. Ranching towns got a lot of drifters.

But did I look like a drifter?

"Sure do," she said.

"Okay. I'd like to see what you have."

She waved at one of her coworkers to take her place and grabbed keys out of a drawer. "Follow me."

We walked outside the grocery and up an exterior set of stairs to a long hallway reminding me of the Motel 6 I'd stayed at during my cross-country drive. Except, the Motel 6 had been nicer.

There were flies buzzing around an unfinished fast-food burger left on the top stair, and cigarette butts scattered outside several doors. The woman took no notice of it besides stepping over them.

"Here we go," she said, putting one of the keys on her lanyard into the flimsy lock on number eight.

I should have just left right then, but my options were limited, if not non-existent. I flicked on a light switch, illuminating a bare bulb that hardly made a difference in a dim room smelling slightly of stale cigarettes and cat pee.

Careful not to touch anything, I walked over to the kitchen. The counters were covered in mouse poop.

Was she fucking kidding?

And what about me? Was I fucking kidding? Was this what life had in store for me? Cigarette butts and mouse crap?

And I'd thought New York was tough.

On the verge of gagging, I darted for the door, and just before I passed through it, the woman held her hands up, confused.

"Where ya going? Isn't it cute?"

Oh, where to start. "I'm not big on mouse poop. And urine smells. But thanks."

She waved her hand. "Oh, that cleans up real easy. Every tenant just comes in and makes the place their own. You know what I mean?"

"Neato. I'll think about it," I called over my shoulder as I ran to the stairs.

Stepping over the unfinished burger.

6
____

RUBY

When I was back in my car, I took long, slow breaths to calm my racing pulse. Was that the best Flood Creek had to offer? If so, I was screwed. Royally screwed.

And speaking of being screwed, a big, black pickup truck had pulled up to the light across the intersection from where I sat in my parked car.

In it was James Everett.

My high school sweetheart.

Jesus, he was still in town?

His arm dangled out his open window, and he tapped the side of his truck in time to the music he was playing.

I sank down in my seat as he passed, and saw he was also singing. He looked happy.

And handsome.

Talk about burning bridges. Just after high school graduation, I'd broken things off with him and left town without looking back. My mother had hounded me for ages to pick up the phone and call him, but I didn't see the point. I was *going places.* And he'd made it clear that he didn't want to go with me.

I doubted he had much in the way of warm feelings for me, so with a pounding heart, I ducked down even further as he drove past. I supposed I'd eventually run into him if I stuck around town, but I didn't want to be trying to explain myself to him before I got my shit together.

I was glad to see he looked happy. He probably had a wife and a kid or two, a good job judging by the nice truck he was driving, and a cute little home on the outskirts of town. He deserved to be happy.

I continued my drive around town, passing my old school and the 4-H Center, finding myself back at what was left of the Flood Creek Hotel. And of course, the saloon just next door.

Oh, what the hell.

I parked at a metered spot, which I didn't bother putting any change in, because no one wrote parking tickets in Flood Creek.

Pulling open the heavy saloon door, I had to wait a moment for my eyes to adjust to the dim interior light.

And when they did, I realized nothing had changed. Not. A. Thing.

I grabbed a seat and rested my elbows on the scarred, wooden bar that ran the length of the room.

"Look who it is," the bartender exclaimed.

I knew him. I was sure of it.

But what was his name?

"Hey, good to see you," I lied.

He put a paper coaster in front of me. "Long time no see. Word has it your parents sold everything and left town."

Was I the last person to get this news?

"Yup. They're gone."

"So are you back for a visit? Say, why're you here if your parents aren't?"

To think I'd come in for just a quiet drink.

I'd forgotten how nosy people were in small towns. "Hey, can I see your list of wines?"

He tilted his head like I'd asked him something in a foreign language. "'Scuse me?"

"Do you have any... oh never mind, I'll have a beer. Whatever you have on tap."

Jesus. Had I really just asked for a wine list?

He smiled. "You sure you don't want something stronger? In case you forgot, we've got more types of whiskey than any other bar in the county."

I'd forgotten that was the saloon's claim to fame.

"I'll start with a beer. Thank you."

He waved over some of the people playing darts. "Guys, guess who's back. Ruby Lee Whitaker. In the flesh."

I was suddenly surrounded by five or six people looking at me like I was some kind of celebrity.

If they only knew.

"Hi, guys. Good to see everyone," I said.

"Hey, weren't you living in the Big Apple?" one of them asked.

I nodded. Here come the lies.

"Yeah. I left because... I wanted to do something different."

That sounded so much better than *I ran away when things got too tough* or *my psycho boss canned me.*

"You look real different, Ruby Lee."

I wasn't sure if that was a compliment or insult, so I just raised my glass. "Cheers."

The bartender chimed in. "I was trying to find out why she came back when her parents aren't here, but she ain't saying much."

I scowled at the bartender, who was slowly ruining his chances at any sort of tip.

Oh fuck it. "You know what? I will take some whiskey. On the rocks."

One drink later, I was regaling people with stories of New York fabulousness, and had even challenged a couple guys to a game of darts.

I stumbled back to the bar for another drink.

"Ruby Lee, you are drinking on the house tonight, that's how happy we all are to have you back."

Now that would *never* happen in New York.

"Thank you. That is very kind..."

Shit. I still didn't know his name.

But I kept babbling, anyway. "You know, I couldn't wait to get out of this shit town back in the day. And now here I am, right where I started."

Oops. Did I really just say that?

Everyone stopped talking and turned to look at me.

A hand gripped my elbow. "I think you've had enough. I'll take you home."

"What? Who do you think you are—"

Oh. Shit.

"James," I said.

The bartender leaned over. "He goes by Jameson now, darlin'."

"Jameson?" I repeated.

My high school sweetheart. In the flesh.

"I'll take you home, Ruby Lee."

I yanked my arm out of his grip, my gaze glued to his. I wanted to look away, but I couldn't. Sure, I'd seen him earlier today when he rolled by in his truck, all happy and jamming out to country music, but now that I was seeing him close up—well, that was a different story. He'd been handsome by any measure when we were teenagers, but a few years' worth of maturing had made him positively beautiful. A thinner face defined his masculine jawline, and the new crinkles around his eyes made him seem like he'd seen a thing or two in his life.

Yeah, that teenaged James was gone.

Enter, grown up James*on*.

He even smelled good, like regular soap and a slight bit of manly perspiration.

Down girl.

I'd never understood why he'd wanted to go out with me in high school. He was so good looking and I was borderline dumpy, even though my mother had always assured me I was beautiful on the *inside*.

But I wasn't ready to go home yet. I pointed a finger at him. "First of all, I go by Ruby now. Dropped the *Lee*. And second, I don't have a home. My parents sold it. I'm home*less*."

He pressed his lips together and shook his head. "I know all that. Roman told me you're staying at the ranch. I'll take you there."

Roman? He talked to Roman?

I hustled out the door behind him, trying to catch up. "How do you know Roman? And what about my car?"

He turned toward me. "You'll come back and get it tomorrow."

We were silent all the way to the ranch. I was too terrified to ask him anything about himself, and I was sure he hated me too much to do the same.

When we pulled up in front of the house, he watched me fish through my purse. "What are you looking for, Ruby?"

I sighed and glanced at the heavy wooden front door I'd passed through so many times. The one that wasn't mine anymore. "I don't have a key."

I'd not gotten one from Roman.

Actually, he hadn't offered.

Jameson shook his head with a laugh. "Ruby Lee, I doubt that door has been locked in twenty years. C'mon. I'll walk you up."

Right. Another New York-ism I needed to abandon. Locking doors. Security. Looking over my shoulder while I walked at night. Those were not going to go easily.

We got to the front door and Jameson opened it right up.

"See? Told you."

I looked up at him in the porch light, wanting to say something but not knowing where to start. He towered over me, his eyes dark under his heavy brow.

Then I got an idea.

"Come inside with me, Jameson," I said impulsively.

"What? Ruby Lee, do you think that's a good idea?"

The little smile on his face told me he sure did.

Maybe he didn't hate me as much as I'd assumed.

"I think it's a very good idea." I took his hand. "And the name is *Ruby*."

"Yeah. Sorry. But I don't know, Ruby…"

I pressed a finger to his lips. "Shhh. You'd better come in now because tomorrow, when I have my wits about me, will be too late."

Oh my god. Was I doing this? What a way to kick off my new, non-New York life.

I took his hand and he followed without protest, like I'd hoped he would.

The moment we reached my room, I threw my arms around his neck and pressed my lips to his while fumbling with my blouse buttons. I shimmied it off my shoulders and dropped it to the floor, followed by my bra. I started working on my jeans, pulling back from kissing him just long enough to untangle myself from my socks and boots.

"Ruby. What are you doing? What are *we* doing?"

Oh my god. I hadn't thought to check. *Idiot.*

"Shit. Jameson. You aren't married, are you?"

Amusement splashed across his face. "No. I'm not married. Now are you sure you want to do this?"

I wished he'd quit asking that.

I crossed my arms over my chest, self-conscious standing there only in my panties. "Um. Yeah. I do."

He smiled. "Okay then."

I started working on his blue jeans. "Do you have a condom?"

He reached into a pocket and returned with a little gold packet held between his thumb and forefinger.

I pushed him back on my bed, straddling him.

"Damn, girl. When did you get so pushy? New York do this to you?" he asked.

"Shhh." I pulled his jeans down and found him nice and hard. I suddenly had to have him in my mouth to taste the precum on his cockhead.

"Ughhh…" He groaned, gently pushing my shoulders. "You're gonna make me come. Slow down."

"Fine. Suit yourself, James-now-known-as-Jameson." I watched him sheath his very nice erection.

"Why don't you stop talking, Ruby Lee-now-known-as-Ruby?"

Fair enough.

He held his cock upright, and I rubbed myself against it, watching him watch me. I hadn't felt so sexy in I didn't know how long. As much as I enjoyed New York, the men there had always struck me as… *watery*. That was the only way I could explain it. They were *fine*, they were *agreeable*, but almost never anything special. Like water.

Was that part of what had drawn me back to Flood Creek?

But I'd figure that out later. I had more important things at hand.

Jameson slipped inside me just a little, causing me to gasp because I hadn't been with anyone in a while. I also hadn't remembered how big he was. Back in the day, when we were doing it every chance we got, I'd had nothing to compare him to.

Yup. He'd been my first.

"Fuck, Ruby, you feel so good." He groaned as I lowered myself.

When I'd taken all of him, I had to stop to catch my breath. It was like a fire had ignited inside me and was spreading out of control. I shuddered and gasped as I pistoned up and down, until an orgasm hit me like a freight train.

"Oh my god," I whispered.

He pushed his hips up and I fell forward on him, accepting his forceful thrusts, my arms wrapped around his neck for purchase.

"Oh my god, I'm coming again," I murmured in his ear.

"Fuck, so am I," he growled, bucking with an intensified fury, one that I'd never experienced.

When we'd caught our breath, I rolled off him and our limbs entangled in each other's. I fell asleep smiling for the first time in a long time.

7

JAMESON EVERETT

"What are you doing? You have no business being here."

Well, shit. Ruby still wasn't up to speed on all the changes that had taken place at her parents' former ranch.

And there she was, finally out of bed—freshly fucked, sober, and mad as a cut snake. And cute as hell.

She might be back in Flood Creek, but she sure as hell had brought the big city attitude with her. She was wearing what I was pretty sure were called *yoga pants*, and I had to say I'd never seen a chubby teenager turn into something quite so freaking gorgeous. Not that I'd cared about that in high school. I'd been madly in love with her.

Not only was her baby fat gone but so was her frizzy hair. Now smooth and sleek, it looked like something right out of a fashion magazine, cut above her shoulders and swinging around her head.

"Well, good mornin', Ruby Lee. How'd you sleep?"

I gave her my best shit-eating grin. Because I could.

Her chest turned a pretty pink color, which spread up her neck, and by the time it reached her face, was nearly a shade of strangled purple.

She'd better check her blood pressure.

She sniffed. "I slept fine, thank you."

I pointed. "How's the head? You got any pounding going on?"

She lifted her chin. "I'm… okay. I found some fifteen-year-old aspirin in my bathroom medicine closet."

I burst out laughing at that one. Sounded like something my mom did, keep shit around the house for fucking ever.

"Let me know if I can call poison control for you," I laughed.

But she didn't.

"Get your feet off my father's desk," she said, hands on hips.

Cripes. Hadn't this woman pretty much begged me to fuck her not ten hours ago?

"It's not your father's. You know that."

She pursed her lips. She was hot by any measure, but now that she was mad, she was killing me. I adjusted myself in my blue jeans because I couldn't stand the torture any longer.

Good old Ruby Lee Whitaker. My first love, who'd dumped my ass as soon as I no longer served her any purpose. I was over it. Really.

But that didn't mean I wasn't going to torment her all I could.

"You're being awfully grouchy for someone who was begging to be fucked just a few hours ago."

Her eyes widened, and I could swear her face grew even more purple as she looked around to make sure no one else was in hearing proximity.

This was fun. And she deserved every bit of shit I could throw her way.

"I… that's not true. That's not how it happened. At all," she stammered.

For someone who'd been in New York for a time, she sure wasn't as tough as I thought she'd be. She was losing her shit faster than I could fuck with her.

Almost took the fun out of it.

Almost.

Yeah, I could be a dick that way.

She shook her head as if to clear her thoughts. "Why are you here, with your feet up on *Roman's* desk?" she demanded.

"For a homeless person, you're pretty damn rude," I said, moving my feet. "And for your information, I'm Roman's business partner. I own this ranch with him. So this desk is theoretically mine too."

She gasped. Apparently, Roman hadn't filled her in on *everything* she'd missed.

And she'd missed a lot.

"Hey, honey, want some breakfast?" Mary asked, appearing in the doorway.

I craned my neck to see around Ruby. Had Mary heard our friendly exchange? "I'm fine, Mary. Ruby Lee might like a little something to settle her stomach though. Rough night and all that."

Mary clicked her tongue like she always did when she didn't like what was going down and put her hand on Ruby's shoulder. "Sweetie, can I get you something?"

Ruby glared at me, but turned to Mary with a smile. "Thank you, Mary. What you can do is tell me what the hell is going on here."

Her voice got more shrill with every word. Maybe I'd pushed her too far. Actually, fuck it. I hadn't done a thing to her. Her flaky parents had.

Roman had filled me in on how she'd just shown up out of the blue, like she was expecting a damn welcoming committee or something. And when she found out her parents had split town after selling everything they had, she'd been pretty much devastated.

Like Roman, I felt for her. She was in a rough spot.

Not that any of it was my problem.

"Well, honey," Mary started. "Your parents sold. You know that."

She pressed her lips together and took a deep breath. "I know they sold. To *Roman*."

Mary nodded, her face covered in sympathy. She really was a nice woman.

"They did sell to Roman. And Jameson."

Ruby looked up at the ceiling of her father's former

office, and rolled her shoulders like she was trying to keep her shit together.

She looked back at Mary as if I weren't in the room. "Fine. Okay. I get it. And Mary, I would love some coffee and a bagel."

"Oh, honey, we don't have bagels. But I have some nice white bread I can butter for you…" As they headed for the kitchen together, their voices faded.

And as they did, Roman stuck his head in the office. Jesus. The place was busy as a train station. How was I going to get any of my fucking work done?

"What was that all about?" he asked.

I shrugged. "Guess when you briefed her about all the recent changes, you forgot to mention *I* was part of the deal."

He smiled and took a seat opposite the desk. "You're right. Didn't want to push her over the edge with too much information. But she's figuring it out real fast." He rubbed his chin, and I realized he was avoiding my gaze.

"What's up with you, man?" I asked.

Roman looked down at his hands. "From what I just overheard, I'm guessing you slept with her last night. Hers were the words of a woman who was regretting something she'd just done and looking for someone to take it out on."

"Damn, Roman. How'd you get to be such an expert on women?"

He shook his head. "Not sure that I am. So, did you?"

I leaned across the desk, not speaking until he looked at me. "Let's put it this way, we didn't get a lot of sleep."

Roman ran his hands over his face. "You know, the only thing her father and I ever agreed on was what a spitfire she was. Some things just don't change, do they?"

"I don't know about that, Roman. Quite a lot has changed around here. For example, did you get a look at the curves on her? She wasn't packing those when she left Flood Creek."

He threw me a disgusted look, got up, and left.

Since when was he so sensitive?

But I was finally alone. Maybe I could get some work done.

8

JAMESON

"Hey, you want a tour of the property? See what else has changed since your parents sold?"

Yeah, I was throwing her an olive branch. I'd been pretty ruthless with my earlier teasing and now I felt bad.

But only a little.

She looked over from her conversation with Mary.

"Go ahead, honey. I need to start dinner, anyway."

She stared out the window for a moment, considering my offer. "I guess. Sure."

We headed for the door. "If I were you, I'd put on some sturdier clothes. You ain't going to the gym, you know."

She glanced at herself. "Yeah, right. Be right back."

I watched her awesome ass bound up the steps to

the second floor, and glanced around the foyer that I'd spent so much time in as a googly-eyed teenager. At the time, I couldn't believe anyone actually lived in a house like the Whitakers'. And now I owned the son of a bitch.

I'd grown up in a simple tract house with a bedroom for my mom, one for me, and a bathroom we shared. It was the best she could do as a single parent on her schoolteacher's salary, but it was home and I loved it.

Mom still lived there, even though now I had a little money and could get her something nicer. But she wasn't interested in moving.

Too much trouble, she'd said.

So, I'd have to find another way to do something special for her. Like take her on a cruise to the Caribbean or something.

But I could just imagine her saying she had no need to leave Flood Creek, and that the tropics were too damn hot, anyway.

The woman drove me crazy. And I adored her.

"So, Jameson, you bought my father's ranch. How did you swing that?" she asked as I put my truck in gear and started driving.

"I inherited some money from my uncle, my mother's brother, a few years back. Finally found something to do with it."

"Your Uncle Jack? I remember him."

I glanced at her as we bounced over the dirt road leading to the far side of the property. Christ, she'd turned into a beautiful woman.

I narrowly missed a tree before I turned my attention back to driving.

Asshole. Watch the road. Not the woman.

Uncle Jack. My stand-in father. He'd told me Ruby would leave me someday.

I wondered what he'd think of the way things stood now…

"Do you live in the house like Roman does?" she asked.

I laughed. "Hell no. That was a stipulation of the partnership. I like my privacy, so I'm in the bunkhouse."

I looked at her again, waiting for distaste to wash over her face. It didn't take long.

"Oh my god, the bunkhouse is a dump. Please tell me you're not living there."

She had a lot of catching up to do.

After driving for fifteen minutes over a bumpy unpaved road, we came into view of the property's outbuildings—stables, barns, and the bunkhouses where ranch hands usually lived.

Every time I drove the ranch's one road, I marveled at its beauty. There was nothing like a Montana ranch, and there'd been no bigger thrill in my life than being able to buy this one.

"Wow, the stables look nice. Guess you painted them?" she asked when I pulled over outside them.

We'd done a hell of a lot more than that.

"'Course. Your dad had let things get a little run down. I think he was just burned out."

She nodded. "Guess that's why they sold."

I turned in my seat to face her. "Did you know I was working for your dad the last few years?"

Her chin dropped. "No. No, I was not aware of that."

"He was good to me, your father. I miss having him around."

"How did you come to work for him?" she asked, clearly still surprised.

I shrugged. "I needed work and approached him. He said that even though you'd left me high and dry, he'd always liked me and was happy for me to join the team."

She shifted uncomfortably in her seat. "I'm glad it worked out so well for you both. Funny, he never said anything about it to me." She looked out the window at the mountains in the distance.

"And I never left you high and dry, anyway," she quipped.

Why did I go there?

But I wasn't backing down. Facts were facts. "Well. You kinda did. C'mon. Really."

Her head snapped in my direction. "No. That's not how it happened."

She was turning red, reminding me of the warning light on an engine.

Danger, danger.

It was funny, but also irked me. I mean, I was over everything that had happened, but I never liked people who don't own up to their shit.

"Okay, Ruby. Why don't you tell me your version, then?"

She took a deep breath.

Yeah. Try and crawl out of this one.

"I was accepted to college back east, and you didn't want to come with me."

Was that the best she could do?

"Oh my god, that is total bullshit. First off, I don't remember any invitation to join you. And second, how the hell was I supposed to go with you anyway? My mom didn't have that kind of money."

She sniffed. "I *did* ask you to come. Would you have if your family had the money? I didn't really see New York as being your kind of place—"

She was going there. Shit.

So interesting how people could rewrite their history.

I jammed the car into *drive*. "This excursion is over."

I got back on the dirt road and in spite of the dips and potholes, drove like a bat out of hell. I couldn't get this woman out of my truck soon enough.

"You know, Ruby, you think your shit doesn't stink. I saw you last night at the saloon, all puffed up like you'd cured fucking cancer or something. But all you really did was *leave town*. How goddamn hard was that? And now, you're back."

She looked at me in disbelief and turned toward the window the rest of the way back to the house, trying to hide the tears running down her face.

I'd made her cry. But the truth hurts sometimes.

I screeched to a stop in front of the house. "And for the record, Ruby," I said as she jumped out of the truck, "you begged me to fuck you last night. Not the other way around."

She slammed the door so hard the entire truck shook.

Pulse racing, I drove back toward the bunkhouse watching her in the rearview mirror while kicking up a cloud of dust till I couldn't see her anymore.

Shit, I needed to put more than dust between us.

"HEY, MOM," I said over my cell after I'd cleaned up and lit a fire in my living room.

Ruby had missed out on seeing what we'd done with the bunkhouse she'd thought was so dumpy, and I wouldn't be offering her another tour anytime soon. We'd renovated one, converting it to individual suites that had turned out nicer than the cozy cabins at the resorts across the state where people paid five hundred dollars a night to pretend to live like cowboys.

And if all went according to plan, we'd be attracting those same tourists here, sooner rather than later.

"Honey," Mom said, "word has it Ruby Lee is back in town. How about that?"

I heard the hope in her voice. I needed to straighten that out right now.

"Mom, she is back, and Roman's letting her stay in her old room. I don't know how long she'll be here, but she and I are not getting back together. So please get that out of your mind right now. She's as high and mighty as they come, Mom. I don't want anything to do with her."

Jesus. I had enough on my mind with the ranch, our

development plans, and having Ruby underfoot. I didn't need my mother ragging on me.

She sighed. "Sure, honey. Hey, tell her to stop by the school if you would. I'd love to say hi and maybe even have her address a couple of the upper classes about her time back east and in the business world. You think she'd do that?"

That meant I'd need to talk to her, which I didn't see happening any time soon.

"Not sure, Mom. But if I see her, I'll mention it," I lied.

"Uh-huh," she said.

What?

My mother was too damn smart by half. She'd probably figured out that Ruby and I had already slept together.

There were no secrets in this fucking town and my mother had always, somehow, managed to read my goddamn mind.

"Gotta run, Mom. Time to make dinner."

I frequently went up to the main house for a nice dinner made by Mary. But I'd be damned if I was going to sit at a dining table looking at Ruby.

I needed to get her out of my mind, and eventually out of my life.

Shake her off.

Except I knew that was going to be easier said than done.

9

RUBY

"Paris? Oh, I don't think I could pull that off just now, Posey."

Was she fucking kidding? She clearly had no idea, absolutely none, about the shit show my life had turned into.

Fuck me.

She breathed hard into the phone, and I could just see her running across the street against the light to get to happy hour at the latest cool place to hang out.

I used to do things like that too. It had only been a week since I'd fled New York, and it already seemed like ages.

A few days in Montana will do that to you.

"Oh, Ruby, c'mon. You have to come. It will be fabulous. Everyone is going and, well, we *need* you."

Posey had a talent with really laying it on when she wanted something. No one was immune.

"I really want to go, hon, I do. But the timing is just not right."

I wasn't sure it would ever be right again.

"Shit," Posey snapped, "there's a fucking line to get in."

"Well, now you can talk to me longer. How's work?" I asked.

She chuckled. "Now that you ask, I'll tell you Sylvie is kicking herself for letting you go. She's lost. Utterly."

Good. And fuck that bitch too. My psycho, abusive boss could find some other marketing assistant to shit on. It was no longer going to be me.

"You know, Rubes, I bet if you came back you could get more money out of her. Maybe move into my building. The old lady on fifteen just died. I can ask about her apartment for you. It would be so fun," she squealed.

My time in New York had come to a big, fat, screeching, unceremonious end. I'd pretty much been chewed up and spit out. I wasn't enough of a masochist to go back.

But I wasn't telling Posey that. For New Yorkers, there was no currency as valuable as living in Manhattan. If you told any of them otherwise, they'd think you were absolutely insane.

Posey would never understand that I'd had my chance at New York. I gave it a shot, and it didn't work out. I wasn't going back. I couldn't. But I wanted to keep my friends there, especially my BFF Posey.

I'd met her in the bathroom at work. We'd started out working for different companies, and kept running into each other in the ladies' room. She'd invited me to happy hour with her friends, and later got me a job at the firm where she worked.

So, while my professional life in New York had crashed and burned, my social life had been pretty damn sweet. That's the reason I stuck it out as long as I had.

'Course no one in Flood Creek knew that. Anyone who asked, I told them I was back for vacation. That was it. Eventually it would become obvious I wasn't going anywhere, and questions would be asked.

I just hoped by the time that happened, I'd have a good explanation for them.

"So tell me, girl, how are things at your parents' ranch? Are the cowboys as fucking hot as they are on *Yellowstone*?"

"They are, Pose. You have to visit."

I hesitated about telling her the ranch was no longer my parents' and that it wasn't really appropriate for me to invite anyone. I'd cross that bridge when I got to it. Thank god she was going to Paris with the girls instead of pushing them all on a flight to Montana.

"Oh my god, I'd love to visit. I just need to figure out when. I'll get cowboy boots and a hat, and you can teach me to ride." She burst out laughing, and I did too because the image of Posey in ranch gear, and on top of a horse, was something that would likely only ever happen in our imaginations. Posey was strictly a coast girl—East Coast or West Coast—and *flyover country*, as she called it, was not a place she had any interest in. Hot cowboys notwithstanding.

"So, Pose, things have been a little bumpy here since I arrived," I said, hoping to keep her off the topic of Paris.

Of course I wanted to go freaking Paris. Who wouldn't? But what she didn't know, and I was too proud to tell her, was that I'd spent every last cent of my earnings in New York trying to keep up with her and all our friends. Weekends in the Hamptons, designer sample sales, chi-chi yoga studios—that nice New York shit cost a lot of money. When all was said and done, I'd come back to Flood Creek without a red cent to my name.

So that nixed Paris for me. Actually, it nixed any place that wasn't Flood Creek.

"What do you mean bumpy? Did you get in a fight with your mom?" she asked.

Posey always fought with her mother and assumed everyone else did, too.

"No, not exactly…"

I guess the happy hour line she was waiting in was moving extremely slowly, because I had time to tell her about my parents selling the ranch to live the 'RV lifestyle,' Roman letting me crash at the house, having sex with Jameson, and then our big blowup that proved he pretty much still thought I was a horrible person.

"Oh honey, that is some rough shit. Geez, I thought life in New York was brutal. Who knew things on a Montana ranch could get so nasty?"

"Yeah. I gotta figure out what the hell I'm going to do."

"Rubes, come back to New York, dammit. Swallow some of that damn Whitaker pride, get over your stubborn self, and come back. Sylvie will hire you in a second."

That meant she'd pummel me—figuratively—in a second, too. The penalty for essentially giving her the middle finger like I had would be grave. Painful. And long-lasting.

"Holy shit, I'm finally up to the fucking door of this place. It better be goddamn worth it. *And what are you looking at?*" she snapped at some unfortunate person.

She was always doing things like that. Some day she was going to get into it with the wrong person and end up with a broken nail or her hair extensions pulled out.

"I'll let you go, Pose. Love you."

"Love you more!" she sang.

I CREPT down the stairs like I did when I was a kid and didn't want to be caught, in the hope of avoiding, well, anyone. I wasn't certain, but suspected Roman had heard me with Jameson a couple nights before, and to put it mildly—I was mortified.

I mean, how the hell did I ever give in to that Neanderthal, anyway? And the nerve of him to suggest I was the pursuer.

He was bona fide crazy, that's what he was. Like I would throw myself at my high school sweetheart after all these years.

Just ridiculous.

I turned at the bottom of the stairs and scooted into the kitchen without a sound.

So far, so good. It seemed like I had the place to myself, which was what I'd been banking on. I'd heard the front door slam with someone leaving just five minutes before and a pickup truck drive away.

But just in case, I snuck across to the kitchen door and was almost in the clear when—

"Hey. Where ya going?"

Before I'd even whipped around, I knew I'd been busted by Roman.

Shit.

"Oh. Hi, Roman. I was just… uh… going out for a bit."

He frowned. "Why didn't you just use the front door? That's where your car is parked."

I didn't have an answer for that. At least, not one I wanted to share.

Then a huge smile spread across his face, showing off the hotter-than-hell creases in the corners of his eyes like lit Fourth of July sparklers.

God help me.

He came over and patted me on the back. "I was just kidding, Ruby. You can use whatever door you want. But I have to say, you sure as hell look guilty. What'd you do? Kill someone? Rob a bank?"

He dropped his head back and laughed again.

I shrugged, wanting to crawl away and die. "Silly of me, huh?" I said, giving a seriously fake laugh.

"Hey, I heard you were in town looking for a place to stay."

Holy shit did word travel fast.

"Oh yeah. That didn't pan out. But I was planning on going out again today and looking."

He held his hands up like a *stop* sign. "No need, Ruby. You stay here just as long as you want to. This house is way too big. It needs a bit of life in it."

"I don't know, Roman. Are you… are you sure?"

"Absolutely. You're always welcome. And no need to sneak around. Even if Jameson is on the premises."

Shit. He knew.

But we were consenting adults when it came down to it, and it was nobody's goddamn business.

That's what I told myself, anyway.

Roman continued. "And don't even think of offering rent or anything like that. You stay in your room for free. Think of it as payment for all those years you had to put up with your father."

He laughed again.

Wait. Did he just bag on my dad?

But I let it slide. "Wow. Thank you," I said, overwhelmed.

He smiled and opened the fridge, grabbing two waters. "Here you go." He twisted the cap off his and downed his in one, manly swallow.

"Hey, I'm heading into town for some errands before my trip to the livestock auction. Want to join me?" he asked, wiping his mouth with the back of his hand.

Good lord. He stood before me, leaning against the

kitchen counter and damn if he didn't look good in broken-in jeans and wide belt accentuating his flat stomach. His shirtsleeves were rolled up to his elbows, and his forearms were deeply tanned and sinewy.

And his jeans perfectly outlined his…

Ugh. Stop. Now.

"You know, Roman, I do need to return my rental car. I think there's an office about a half hour away."

He threw his hands in the air. "Great. Let's go. I'll follow you, and afterwards, we can get a bite at the diner. Whaddya say?"

"I'd say it's a date."

Just a figure of speech. Right?

10

RUBY

"You know," Roman said as we drove away from the rental car office, "you can use one of the ranch trucks if you like. You know, since you returned your car."

I turned to him, and while he concentrated on driving, I was able to check out his profile. Goodness.

"Hey, I don't want to be a freeloader. You can put me to work or something," I offered.

He laughed. "Well, you've already helped one of us," he glanced at me and winked.

Oh god. I faced forward for the rest of the ride.

When my mortification passed, I was able to chitchat again. "It's funny. The house that was mine—well, my parents' and by default mine—no longer is. It's so strange. Just the weirdest feeling," I said, watching the rolling hills whiz by.

Roman rested his hand on mine, sending a shockwave through me. "Like I said, it's your place too, for as long as you want."

"That's… very kind," I sputtered.

The streets in town were busy as lunchtime approached—or, as busy as the streets in Flood Creek got, anyway—and as we walked from our car a couple blocks to the diner, several of the women we passed made sure to say a very friendly hello to Roman.

Well, I'd be damned. He had ladies throwing themselves at him.

"Hey, Roman," a pretty blonde called after him.

"Hello," he responded with a half-hearted wave, not even turning around.

I wasn't surprised. When I was a teenager, a popular nickname for Mr. Maxwell had been "DILF."

He'd always been freaking gorgeous.

Fun fact. The first man I'd ever seen naked was Roman. Not that he knew that.

I'd arrived early to babysit one evening, and let myself in the house. While wandering around looking for the kids and Mrs. Maxwell, Mr. Maxwell was walking around his bedroom butt naked, with the door wide open.

And did I run in the other direction, mortified by my finding, like any other nice girl? Hell no. I stood behind a column and watched until I heard Mrs. Maxwell and the kids come in the back door.

No one ever knew.

But it was my first look at a penis. I hadn't even seen my dad's or brother's. Nope, my first was Mr. Maxwell.

Wonder what he'd say if I shared that little tidbit with him.

WHEN WE WERE SEATED and had ordered, and everyone in the diner had said hello to Roman, and many of them to me, I realized I didn't know much about the man. My dad had always claimed that because Roman hadn't grown up in ranching, he was little better than a dilettante. A dabbler. An amateur.

Yup. Even ranchers could be snobby.

"Roman, how'd you get into ranching?"

He leaned toward me, and damn if I couldn't feel his heat. I took a gulp of my ice water. I would have rubbed a cube over the back of my neck if it wouldn't have been so obvious.

He lowered his voice. "It's a secret." He sat back, smiling.

As soon as I realized he was kidding around, I called him out. "Yeah, right. Spill it."

He picked a fry off my plate. "It's pretty simple, really. My ex-wife was from a ranching family, and she wanted to raise our kids the same way she'd grown up. So, I agreed to give it a shot. I loved it. And… look at me now." He dove into his double cheeseburger.

"Oh. That makes sense," I said, taking a spoonful of my tomato soup.

Another New York habit. I only ate a real meal at dinner. The rest of the day was little more than snacks. Like soup.

Roman was so easy to talk to, curious about me and interested in what I had to say. It didn't take long to realize that all the shit my dad had said about him over the years was just that—shit.

When we got back to the house, it smelled heavenly. Dinner was hours away, but Mary was cooking something amazing like she always did.

"Thanks for lunch and the ride, Roman," I said as he headed for his office and I to my room.

"Hey, before you go." He gestured that I come over. "I told you a secret. Now you owe me one."

Huh?

"I don't really have…"

And before I knew it, his lips were on mine, firm and tasting like the mint he'd popped in the car.

"Mmmm," he murmured as he pulled away.

But I wasn't done. If he could steal a kiss, so could I. I put my hands on either side of his gorgeous face and returned my lips to his—

Someone banged into the kitchen from the side door. I craned my neck from the foyer to see who it was, and looked back at Roman, my heart thudding.

"What is he doing here?" I asked quietly, my hands dropping from his face.

Roman's eyebrows rose. "Cam? Well, he's one of our business partners. It's the three of us—Jameson, Cam, and myself."

Camden Emmanuel. My brother Bud's best friend.

He owned Flood Creek Ranch now too?

11

CAMDEN EMMANUEL

"HEY, ROMAN, I WANTED TO TALK TO YOU ABOUT—"

I blew around the corner to find my business partner in the office where he usually hung out.

What the hell?

There he stood with Ruby Lee Whitaker. Daughter of the former owners of Flood Creek Ranch.

Of all people. Where in god's name had she come from?

We stared at each other like we were looking at ghosts.

She was the first one to recover. More or less.

She scowled at Roman, who she was standing close to. *Very* close to. "Are there any other owners of my parents' ranch that I should know about? Like maybe the mayor? The bartender at the saloon? Or how about the lady at the grocery who owns the disgusting apartments above the store?"

Her voice got more strident with each word. I usually bailed when women reached this point. I was a chicken shit when it came to female emotions. But I was too shocked to move.

Even Roman had a little deer-in-the-headlights thing going on.

"Ruby Lee. Hello," I stammered.

She kept looking at Roman, like if she ignored or just plain didn't acknowledge me, I might not really be there.

"It's nice to see you, Ruby Lee."

What else could I say?

And what had she been doing standing so close to Roman when I'd come around the corner?

Actually, scratch that. I didn't want to know. I didn't do drama and wanted no part of anyone else's.

But first things first.

She finally tore her gaze from Roman and greeted me with what I could only call a world-class stink eye.

I couldn't remember the last time I saw her. Must have been when she was still in high school, or shortly thereafter. My best friend's kid sister.

Well, former best friend.

She looked good. Real good. Wonder if Jameson had seen her yet. He was going to be pleased.

"So you own the Flood Creek Ranch too, Cam?" she sniffed.

I cleared my throat. "Um, yes, I do, Ruby Lee. Your

father sold to the three of us. I have a smaller share than Roman or Jameson… Wait, did you know Jameson was a partner, too? You remember him, don't you, your high school boyfriend—"

"Yes, I know who Jameson is," she snapped. "And yes, I know he's one of the ranch's new owners. I just didn't know there was a *third* partner."

Roman clapped his hands. "I got lucky with these two guys. Great business partners."

Ruby Lee's stink eye moved from me to him. He either didn't notice, or ignored it.

I needed to learn to do that.

So I tried to move the subject from me to her. "Ruby Lee, what brings you here?" I asked, hoping she wouldn't bite my head off.

Her chin quivered. Shit. I hated it when a woman cried.

She took a deep, indignant breath. "I left New York, drove all the way to Montana to surprise my parents, but it turned out the surprise was on me. Or should I say, the joke was on me. They sold the goddamn place without telling me."

Her voice started to crack. The tears were on their way. I knew how girls were. Once they started, the flood was close behind.

"Are you kidding? Your parents actually did that?"

Wow. I didn't take the Whitakers for pulling some-thing like that.

Roman put his hands up. "To be fair, *they* wanted to surprise *her* at the same time and were on their way to

New York when she got here."

Surprises all around.

"Just like two ships passing in the night," he laughed.

"Well, shit, Ruby Lee. I'm sorry to hear that."

And... that was the tipping point I'd seen coming. Next thing I knew, she ran toward me and pressed herself against my chest, covering her face with her hands.

What in the fucking fuck?

I looked at Roman and waved my hands in a *what do I do?* fashion.

He just shrugged in return.

Thanks, pal.

So I put my hands on her shoulders, and as soon as I did, she heaved with sobs.

Goddammit. When I got up this morning, I sure wasn't expecting to have to comfort a distraught female.

After a minute, I gently pulled her away far enough to see her tear-stained face.

Christ, did she look sad. Actually, not even sad. She was broken. Just freaking broken. Why the hell was she taking all this so hard? Sure, it sucked to have your parents sell your childhood home, but this reaction seemed extreme.

"Ruby Lee, pull yourself together," I said, trying to get her to look at me.

She stepped away and turned her back to us, sniffling and wiping her eyes on her sleeve.

Well, shit.

I put an arm around her shoulders. After all, she was

my former best friend's kid sister. I'd pretty much watched her grow up.

Maybe changing the subject would help. "Hey, Ruby Lee, how's your brother, Bud?"

She took a deep breath and glanced up at me. "Sorry about all this, Cam. I guess I've been overwhelmed with things lately. My brother—well, I haven't been in touch with him in a while."

Interesting.

She looked back at me, confused. "Why? You haven't been in touch, either? That's surprising."

Lots of surprises today, it turns out.

"Um, yeah. We um… we kind of lost touch. Long time ago, when he left town."

She looked at me, her face red and puffy, and frowned. "Are you serious? I didn't know. He left ages ago."

I nodded. "Yup. He sure did."

It wasn't the right time to continue a conversation about Bud. Actually, it might never be a good time to talk about Bud. So, I took the opportunity to get the hell out of there.

"Hey, I got some work to see to at the outbuildings. We'll catch up later, huh?" I said, hustling out the door like my ass was on fire.

12

CAM

NEXT MORNING, I ENTERED BY THE KITCHEN SIDE DOOR just as I saw Ruby taking off in one of the ranch trucks. Roman saw me watching.

"Well, that was something yesterday, wasn't it?" I asked.

Mary nodded as she served us both some coffee.

"Eh, she's just going through a rough patch," he added. "She'll be fine. Eventually."

Christ, I hoped so.

"Where'd she go in the truck?" I asked.

Mary piped in as she placed a mound of scrambled eggs and bacon on a huge serving platter in front of us like she did every morning. "She took a job delivering flowers."

She took a job? Okay. She clearly wasn't here for a quick visit home. Not that it was her home anymore.

"No shit. She's going to work for Erin? That should be interesting."

Erin, the owner of the town's floral shop, was not known to be an easy person to work for. But hell, Ruby Lee had just spent several years in New York. I'd heard everyone there was a hardass. Maybe she'd fit right in.

"And by the way, she doesn't go by Ruby Lee anymore. Now it's just *Ruby*," Mary added.

Okay. Big city girl changes her name. Nothing wrong with that.

I'd always known that Ruby Lee—Ruby—wanted to get the hell out of Flood Creek. Yeah, she was a rancher's daughter and all that that entailed, but she'd always had a curiosity the average Flood Creek kid just didn't possess.

Myself included.

And Jameson included, too. Her high school boyfriend, poor guy, couldn't keep up with her and was basically left in the dust. Not that he really even tried. I think he'd seen the writing on the wall. At least, that's what the town gossip had whispered.

The kitchen door slammed, and Jameson joined us in the breakfast nook, settling in and helping himself to a healthy serving of Mary's cooking.

When I'd bought into the ranch with the other guys, I hadn't realized meals—and I mean damn good meals— were included in the deal. What a fucking bonus that turned out to be. I'd never eaten so well in my life.

"Dude," I said, "you know Ruby Lee's back in town, huh?"

Jameson's face darkened.

Shit. Should have kept my mouth shut.

"Yup. Her name is *Ruby* now. And yes, I know she's back," he snarled.

I looked out the kitchen window, watching one of the ranch hands clean brush away from the house. It seemed like I'd spent my entire youth here at the Whitaker ranch, hanging out with and getting into trouble with Bud. And now I *lived* here. Drama aside, I couldn't believe how lucky I was.

My old friend might be out of my life, but the ranch sure wasn't. Most days I pinched myself when I woke up in the morning.

Roman glanced at his wristwatch while Mary delivered more bacon. She knew us well.

"Guys, we all have a lot to do today, so I'd like to kick off the meeting."

Jameson and I nodded and gave him our attention. As the majority investor, he was the default leader of the group. Which was fine with me. I'd had some money, two strong arms, and a lot of construction knowledge to contribute, but I didn't know shit about running a business.

"Can you bring us up to date on the permits?"

We both looked at Jameson, who pressed his lips together and shook his head slowly. "Not much progress has been made there. The planning board is really digging their heels in."

Roman rubbed the back of his neck, then slammed his fist on the table, startling Mary so badly she dropped a cast iron pan.

"Roman. Please don't do that," she scolded.

He waved in her direction. "Sorry, Mary. Sometimes I forget my manners."

He turned back to us. "That fucking pisses me off. There's no reason we shouldn't be able to develop the property according to the plans we've provided the board. We're ready to go with roads, water, power—the works. And still, they stonewall us."

Jameson drummed his fingers on the table. He'd taken the lead on working with the planning board, and it clearly weighed on him there hadn't been more progress.

We were a good team that way, not wanting to let the others down.

"I'm not sure what else to do, guys. It seems like the powers that be don't want us turning the ranch into a visitor destination. Even on the small scale we compromised with."

No one said anything, but it was pretty much a foregone conclusion that the resistance on the part of the zoning board had to do with them not liking Roman. To them, he'd always been an outsider who didn't understand the way things were done. And it didn't help that his years of battling with Whit Whitaker had pitted some people against him, and others against Whit.

Unfortunately, most of the old dudes on the planning board were guys Mr. Whitaker had grown up with.

I'd always liked Mr. Whitaker. He and his wife had

included me in many a family activity since I didn't get that from my own. But he'd sure done a number on Roman Maxwell.

Whit Whitaker was one person you just didn't want to piss off. Years later, Roman was still paying the price.

"Shit, shit, shit," he mumbled.

If our permits didn't come through, and we couldn't develop Flood Creek the way we planned to, I was fucked. Totally fucked. I'd sunk every penny I had—it wasn't much, but it was ten years of savings—to buy my share. I was going to manage most of the building construction on the ranch. Without that, I didn't have a whole lot to offer. And there likely wouldn't be any money to buy back my share, if one of the guys wanted to.

My big breakfast suddenly wasn't sitting too well in my stomach, as the realization struck that I might have hitched my horse to the wrong wagon.

Don't get me wrong. I had a world of respect for Roman and Jameson. I considered them my friends. But I was wondering more and more if I'd taken a risk I should not have.

We sat in silence until Mary brought over some toast and homemade preserves.

"So, Ruby was coming here to visit her parents. Why'd she take a job? Isn't she going back to New York?" I asked.

Roman and Jameson shrugged. "That remains to be seen. She's being cagey about answering."

Odd.

"Well, she sure looks good, doesn't she?"

The guys looked at each other.

Oh shit. That was a sure sign something was up.

I lowered my voice so Mary couldn't hear. "What the hell? Is someone dating her? Already?"

Jameson dug into his toast like he hadn't heard the question. But Roman wasn't letting him off the hook.

"She and Jameson had a little fun the other night," he said.

I *knew* it. "No shit, dude. And what about you, Roman? Didn't I walk in on a little something yesterday? You two had *guilty* written all over your faces."

Jameson shot him a look. "Seriously, Roman?" he asked.

He shrugged. "She's a beautiful woman, boys. And I'm not the possessive type. You're welcome to get to know her any way you want, as long as she's into it."

Jameson rolled his eyes. "You can both fucking have her. She's a big pain in the ass."

"Ooooh, Jamie's got his panties in a twist," Roman teased.

I leaned closer. "What happened? C'mon. Spill it."

"We got in a big fight about why we broke up. It was ugly. And I suppose, stupid, too." He gave one of those *no big deal shrugs* that meant anything but.

Well, well. Little Ruby Lee Whitaker was all grown up. And for once, no one had a claim on her. At least not much of a claim.

The truth was, I'd always had a thing for my best friend's

little sister. But I'd been late to the game, again and again. By the time I'd worked up the courage to ask her out, Jameson had beaten me to it. And their high school romance had been legendary. The kind movies were made about.

Until she left, that was.

Probably just as well. Her brother would have killed me if I'd tried to date her. So I asked out another girl and we became an item, even though my heart wasn't completely in it.

And boy, did that shit crash and burn.

IT WAS darts night at the Flood Creek Saloon, and I was in second place in the tournament. It was the furthest I'd ever gone. 'Course, I'd been practicing my ass off in the barn at the ranch. Not that anyone knew that.

And who did I find when I arrived, fairly well into her cups, but Ruby—formerly known as Ruby Lee.

"Hey there," I said, grabbing the stool next to her at the bar.

"Cam," she exclaimed with a slight slur.

Damn, she hadn't wasted any time.

"I understand you're delivering flowers for Erin. How's that going?"

She pushed her hair behind her ears and sat up a little straighter. "It was totally fucked, if you must know the truth. Only one person tipped me this morning. The bastards in this town are seriously cheap."

I tried not to smile, but her indignation was damn funny.

"Go ahead. Laugh. Whatever. I deserve it."

"I'm heading to the back for the darts tournament—" I started to say as I got up from my seat.

She waved her hand like she didn't hear me. "I delivered flowers to two people from high school who just had babies, and to one person whose wedding is the day after tomorrow. All these people making shit happen in their lives. And look at me."

I wasn't sure what she was getting at. I wasn't sure I wanted to know.

"And now my back aches from being in the truck all day. Don't get me wrong, it's very nice of Roman to let me use it. I just have to get used to the suspension." She buried her face in her hands.

Well, shit.

"Ruby. You need to go home. C'mon. I'm taking you."

So much for darts.

Without any resistance, she shrugged and grabbed her purse. I threw some money on the bar to cover her beers.

"I'm sorry, Cam. I'm a downer, aren't I?"

I held the door for her. "You're going through a rough patch. It happens to all of us."

God knew I'd had my share of hard knocks.

"Thank you, Cam."

She chattered about New York on the quick ride home, and when we pulled up in front of the house, I got out with her.

"Thanks so much for the ride, Cam. I'll see you tomorrow, probably," she said when we reached the front door.

"I'm coming in too, Ruby."

Confusion washed over her face. "You are?"

I nodded. "Yeah. I live here."

She lowered her chin and stared at me like she was possessed. "Are you fucking kidding me?"

Where the hell did she think I lived? It was my house now. Well, along with Roman and Jameson.

"I took your brother's old room. Although that twin bed sucks."

She smirked. "Tell me you're not sleeping in that horrible thing. That was my bed growing up. When Bud left, I traded it out for his double. Why didn't you just take my room?"

I pushed the front door open and we walked toward the stairs. "I don't know. Too girly, I guess. Plus, I'd spent so much time in your brother's room as a kid, I just felt more comfortable there."

When we reached her bedroom door, we stopped.

She looked up at me. "Cam, you've been so kind. Thank you for putting up with my breakdowns. I'm getting my shit together. I really am."

I sure hoped so.

"Happy to help. We did grow up together, after all."

She looked around the darkened house. "You know, Cam, I always had a bit of a crush on you."

Thanks for waiting all these years to clue me in.

"Well, um, I might have had a little crush on you too," I said.

Shit. I wished I hadn't said that. I needed to keep my thoughts to myself.

And before I could turn away to head to my own room, Ruby's arms were around my neck. She tilted her head and looked at me as if she were offering an invitation.

So why the fuck not? I lowered my lips to hers and damn if years of dreaming about her didn't slam into me with the satisfaction of finally, finally, having the chance to kiss her.

13

RUBY

"RUBY LEE! HEY, RUBY LEE!"

I'd know that voice anywhere. Melanie Belters. And while I loved my high school BFF, something told me this reunion was going to be painful.

I forced a smile on my face and turned around. "Melanie," I cried, trying to match her enthusiasm.

She ran at me and threw her soft arms around my shoulders, squeezing until I was bound, as if in a strait-jacket. The top of her curly head came only to my chin, so her embrace was like being tackled by a miniature football lineman.

In spite of myself, it was lovely to see her. We'd been inseparable growing up, and while our lives had taken different paths, she'd never been insulted that I'd moved on from Flood Creek. There were many times I wished she had come to the East Coast with me.

Instead, at the age of twenty-eight, she had a houseful of children ranging in age from six months to eight years. And she and her husband weren't done yet.

How do I know all this? Melanie, bless her, had always been careful to keep my most up to date address, dropping me a newsy note every now and then about her life, her kids, and if she were feeling generous, her husband.

I didn't deserve her.

"Girl, I heard you were back in town. And I was thinking to myself, I was thinking *why hasn't that bitch called me yet?*" She dropped her head back and cackled loudly enough to be heard down the block.

She was truly one of a kind, confident in her skin in a way few people were. I supposed that's why she wasn't bothered by my leaving town, and in fact was always so supportive. She knew deep down, staying in Flood Creek was where she belonged, and that someplace else was right for me. It was a simple black and white fact, and she didn't spend too much time analyzing it.

"Hey, Mel. I was planning to call, I really was. I just wanted to get some things organized first."

It was only a sort-of lie.

She waved her hand as if dismissing a fly. "Organized? There's nothing organized about life, honey. Don't kid yourself."

She had a point. She wasn't a planner, and yet she

somehow always figured out how to take the bull by its horns.

I don't know that Melanie had put a lot of thought into how many kids to have, nor how she and her husband would take care of all of them. It was just a foregone conclusion, the way the sun came up every day, that they'd have as many as their zesty sex life gave them, and that everything would somehow work itself out. And it would, because things worked out for Melanie.

I was so not like that.

"Oh Jesus, what now?" she mumbled, fishing her cell phone out of her purse. "What?" she barked.

After several *uh-huhs* and *no, don't do thats*, she hung up.

"Goddamn husbands. I don't know who is more work —him or the kids. With as helpless as he is, you'd never guess we're on child number four."

Shaking her head, she clicked her tongue.

"But, Ruby Lee, let me look at you," she said, turning me like I was a mannequin. "Mmmm hmmm. You filled out nice, honey. Got some titty action up top, thank god. Jesus, we thought you'd be flat as a pancake for life. Oh, and you got that flat tummy and a nice little ass. I can't believe some guy ain't snapped you up yet."

Well, I *had* kissed three different guys in as many days, who not only were business partners, but who also happened to own my parents' former ranch.

"Yeah, well, I'm kind of in transition, Mel."

She reached up and flicked the ends of my chin-length bobbed hair. "Hmmm. Guess your hairdresser was feeling a little punk rock last time you saw him, huh? Well, don't worry, it will grow back." She cackled.

Punk rock? I was pretty sure the punk rock era had bypassed Flood Creek. But whatever.

"Darlin', are you back for a funeral or somethin'?"

"What? No. Why?" I stammered.

She looked me up and down. "Well, honey, you're wearing all black."

I looked down at my black jeans and T-shirt. Another New York-ism. Wearing black was easy, and didn't show subway dirt. I glanced up and down the street and realized all the other women were wearing bright colors and florals.

I might have had one pair of panties with flowers, which my friends had bought me as a joke. Florals weren't really my thing.

Well, shit.

"I guess I kind of stick out, huh?"

"Oh, honey, you're a rose among thorns. But I'd say you could stand to brighten things up a bit. I have a friend who's hosting a LuLaRoe party this weekend. We'll get you suited up with some colorful things. Don't you worry."

LuLaRoe? What the hell was that?

I was aching for some sympathy. "So I guess you heard my parents sold?"

Her eyes widened, and she nodded. "Oh yes. It was the talk of the town. They packed up and got the hell out of Dodge, as they say. I heard you didn't find out till you arrived. Must have come as quite a shock."

She had no idea.

"It's been crazy. That's for sure."

She put her hands on her hips. "So how long you in town for?"

Ugh. I still didn't have a good answer to that question. Or a bad one.

"Not sure, Melanie."

She patted my arm. "The reason I'm asking is that, well, you probably already know, but I'm chairwoman of our high school reunion committee, and we are planning quite the bash. I'd love it if you could join the group. We could really use some new blood."

She looked around conspiratorially. "We also got all them bitchy girls from the cheerleading squad on the committee always trying to take over and pull their mean girl shit, but you know me. I smack them down so hard they don't know what hit them. It'd be great to have someone to fight them off with."

She looked at me with so much hope, I wanted to say yes.

But I wasn't sure a high school reunion committee was for me. I didn't even know if a high school reunion itself was something I could stomach.

"Melanie, I gotta run. Erin is waiting for me to do some flower deliveries this morning."

"Oh my goodness." She fake-smacked the side of her face. "You're working for Erin. Well, good luck with that." She dropped her head back and laughed again.

I threw my arms around her. Melanie was a lot, but sometimes you needed a lot to snap you out of your rut.

"I'll see you soon then?" I asked.

"Abso-fucking-lutely, Ruby Lee. You'll come for dinner next week. Here, put your digits in my phone." She nudged me and giggled. "That's what the kids say these days."

14

____

RUBY

I DIDN'T KNOW WHY PEOPLE WERE SO INTIMIDATED BY Erin. She gave me her flower orders and I delivered them. It was no more complicated than that.

Made me wonder who the hell had worked for her in the past. The work wasn't exactly brain surgery. Plus, she gave me free flowers. Granted, they were the ones with broken or bent stems. But when I brought them home and put them in a vase, they looked fine, reminding me of how my mother had kept the house stocked with fresh flowers when they were in season.

Speaking of my parents, I was a little less pissed at them every day. I couldn't blame them for moving on. It was their life and their ranch. They deserved some adventure after all their years of working so hard. But the night before, when I was fishing through the hall credenza for some matches to light a candle, I came across an old box of photos.

I took it back to my room, and sat on the rug. While my parents had sold the house with its contents, they'd removed their most personal effects. They must have missed this particular box, stuffed in the back of an old piece of furniture.

It was funny, finding family photos, a literal snapshot of a moment in time. There were pictures of my mom and Mary cooking, my dad putting finishing touches on a new barn, and my brother and me climbing a tree where one of the ranch hands had built us a little fort.

The usual lump built in my throat, but I swallowed it away. I was tired of crying. I was lucky to have grown up on the ranch, lucky to have tried life in New York, and lucky to be back. I didn't have a damn thing to gripe about.

I needed to keep reminding myself of that, and stop being a whiny little bitch.

Yeah, right. We'll see how long that lasts.

I pushed the box under my bed next to my duffel bag and suitcase before I went to bed. When the time came to leave the ranch, there was no way it could be forgotten this time.

Since I was done with my flower deliveries early so I decided to take a walk around town. I was amazed at how many of the mom and pop stores I'd grown up with had been replaced with boring chains like dollar stores and 7-Eleven. It was kind of sad, but who was I to judge? I'd left town just like the mom and pops had. I hadn't felt obligated to stick around, just like they hadn't.

I passed by the grocery store with the nasty apartments above them, and ducked in to see if I could find something to bring back to the ranch I thought everyone might like.

"Can I help you, sweetie?" the clerk asked. "Oh. You're the one I showed the apartment to the other day. I hate to tell you, but the place is gone. Was snapped up right fast."

Holy crap.

"Glad to hear it. Hey, can you tell me where the bagels are?"

I'd been jonesing for a good one since I'd left New York.

The clerk frowned, and tapped her chin with her forefinger. "You know, we had some of those last year. But we never got any more."

What? No bagels. Where the fuck had I landed?

"But we have Entenmann's powdered donuts over there, and English Muffins are on sale right next to them."

"Okay."

I continued my wandering and came across the old movie theater. It was not only still standing but also operational. And by some stroke of fortune, the guy in the ticket booth was the same man who'd run the place when I was growing up.

"I remember you," I said to him.

I'd always thought he was so old, but now I realized he probably wasn't much older than my parents.

He leaned toward the mic in his booth, which he really didn't need. It wasn't like downtown Flood Creek was teeming with noisy activity. "Aren't you one of the Whitaker kids?" he asked.

Oh my god. He remembered.

"Yes. I am. I'm back to visit. But my parents moved away."

He nodded. "Yep. I heard that."

Jesus. I really *was* the last to find out.

"How did you stay open all these years?" I asked. "So many other businesses are gone."

He raised his eyebrows. "Honey, I own this whole damn block."

No fucking way. He'd always dressed like a homeless person and rode around on a rusty bicycle.

Good for him.

"Mind if I go in to take a peek?" I asked.

He looked behind me as if being permissive might tick off another patron. Even though there was no one around.

He nodded toward the doors. "All right. Go ahead. But if you stay long enough to watch a movie, you're gonna have to pay for it."

"I'll only be a few minutes. Promise."

I pushed open the ornate theater doors and was instantly transported back to my teen years, when the guy in the booth—whose name I didn't even know— would let us into R-rated movies even when we weren't old enough. The same threadbare carpet covered the floor, and the display case of the long-closed-up concession stand was full of dust bunnies and crumpled napkins.

But somehow, it still smelled like popcorn and the same slight mustiness it had back then.

I pulled the door open a crack to the one movie that was playing and in the cool darkness saw the shadow of a single head in front of a brightly lit screen, blasting some Western movie I'd never heard of.

I walked back outside, squinting in the sunlight. "Thanks for letting me take a look. I'm glad you're still here."

"Me too, missy, me too."

I turned to continue on my walk when I spotted Jameson at the end of the block, chatting up a pretty blonde.

Figured. I knew he was just a man whore.

In spite of that, I had to admit he was way hotter than any of the soft guys I'd met in New York City, with his jeans hanging low around his hips, scuffed cowboy boots, and his tan, buff physique.

Damn him.

15

ROMAN

"Well, look who we have here. The Flood Creek Ranch trio."

I looked up from my burger, followed by Jameson and Cam, to see our table being visited by Tilda Burke, the mayor's wife and nosy town gossip.

In a small town like Flood Creek, everyone gossiped about everyone else. You could hardly take a shit without someone from the next valley over knowing. And, of course, commenting on it.

That's one of the things that had surprised me when I first moved to Flood Creek with my then-wife. It wasn't so much that people talked—I understood that because it was a pretty tight-knit community—but they didn't even try to hide that they were all into each others' business.

In a more cosmopolitan setting people might gossip, but they always pretended not to.

I wasn't sure which was worse. But when my wife left me, there wasn't a person in town who didn't, at some point, come up to me and say something. Just when I would rather have had my private life, private. But that was a small ranching community for you.

I took a swig of beer to prepare for whatever Tilda had to lay on us. Talking about other people was the *only* thing she did.

Her oversized capped teeth reflected the bright diner lighting, making her smile seem outsized and kind of wicked. Or was that just my imagination?

"So, boys," she said with a little shimmy of her shoulders, "I understand the Whitaker girl is back in town. Isn't that funny? Her parents left, but she came back." She giggled, bleached curls bobbing around her head.

She waited for us to spill, but we just looked at her.

When she realized she'd have to work a little harder for some dirt, her smile faded and her lips pressed together in a thin line. "Anybody know why she's back?" she asked expectantly.

I wanted to ask her why the fuck she cared, but my abrasive approach had gotten me into trouble on more than one occasion. So, I kept my mouth shut and looked at the guys.

Cam cleared his throat. "She's visiting," he said, nodding.

Tilda leaned a little closer. "Visiting *who*?" she whispered.

Really lady? If I wasn't working so hard to win over the planning commission, of which her mayor husband was part, I might tell her to hit the road.

Jameson shrugged. "Guess you'll have to ask her."

I was glad all three of us guys were on the same page about keeping Ruby's business quiet. To the extent we could, anyway. Word would eventually get out—that she'd arrived expecting to see her parents, who had left without telling her—but we weren't contributing to the story.

Much to Tilda's chagrin.

"So, where's she staying, since we no longer have a hotel?"

I had a feeling she knew just where Ruby was staying, but wanted to open the door to more innuendo.

"Where should she stay, Tilda?" I asked. "Your house?"

Her eyes grew wide, and her hand flew up to her chest in shock. "Oh. *Well.* Our guest room is under construction. So we couldn't possibly put her up."

Bullshit.

She shifted. "But isn't she staying with you guys?" she asked, her eyes flashing.

"Why are you asking if you already know?"

Her head snapped back at my sharp words. She was finally stumped. The three of us turned back to our dinner, and next time I looked up, she was gone.

Thank god.

"Jesus, that woman is horrible," I said, looking around to make sure she'd really left.

Jameson rolled his eyes. "You haven't been around her and her husband all your life like Cam and I have."

Cam nodded. "My older brothers grew up with them. They've always been pains in the ass."

"What I don't get is why she's so interested in what Ruby is up to."

Jameson rubbed his beard. He'd been trying to grow it forever, and I loved giving him shit about it. "She knows very well that Ruby is staying in the house, and she wants to get as much dirt as possible so she has something interesting to spread."

Maybe that was why people in a small town were so gossipy. There wasn't a hell of a lot going on that was particularly exciting. An attractive, young woman crashing with three single men was something to talk about, I supposed. Something that didn't happen every day.

And something that I was damn happy had happened to us.

THE DAY BEFORE, on my way through town, I'd spotted Ruby standing in the doorway of a boarded-up shop, peeking around the corner at none other than her old beau Jameson. I knew they'd been together years before, so I guess it was natural they were curious about each other.

Their current animosity was unmistakable, that was for damn sure. It was unfortunate, but they'd get past it at some point, I figured. You can only hold grudges for so long. On the other hand, Ruby was a Whitaker, and her father was stubborn as a damn mule. So, maybe not.

I felt a little badly getting a laugh at her expense, but her not-very-discreet spying was funny as hell. She looked none too pleased that Jameson was talking to a very pretty woman.

But Ruby wasn't the only curious person around. *I* was curious about *her*, and becoming more so every day.

After her initial distress over finding her childhood home sold off to three business partners and her parents RVing around the country, she was handling her unexpected circumstances better than a lot of people could. She'd immediately gone looking for a place to live, although I was prepared to do my damnedest to keep her at the ranch, and she'd even found a way to make some money. I was sure it wasn't much, but then there weren't a lot of options in Flood Creek unless you were a cowboy or wrangler.

I was pretty sure that whatever she was doing in New York was not available around here.

I pulled my truck over to watch her watch Jameson, who was now heading down the street with his pretty friend.

It was nothing less than astonishing to see the woman she'd grown into. I didn't know how or where she began her transformation, but there was something about seeing my former chubby, plain-Jane babysitter turn into a sexy, gutsy woman. That tickled me.

Seriously. Every night since she'd arrived I'd gone to

bed thinking of her, and was only able to sleep once I'd rubbed one out, picturing coming all over her pretty tits while she looked up at me with her perfect smile.

What could I say? It had been way too long since I'd been with a woman, and having one like Ruby under my roof was killing me.

And then there was the way she'd kissed me a couple days before. There'd been no hesitation. She had all the confidence of a woman who knew what she wanted, and she wasn't afraid to ask for it.

But she sure had jumped when Cam appeared.

Which was fine with me. I liked her a little uncomfortable and uncertain. Not knowing where the next curve ball would come from. I liked the idea of keeping her guessing.

It was more fun that way, if not a little confusing. My ten-plus years on her was a big spread by any measure, although it didn't seem to bother her. I was freaking forty years old. Actually, almost forty-one.

I was considering getting out of the truck to ask her to coffee when a couple guys stopped to talk to her. One tall and one short.

From the look of it, I guessed it wasn't going to be too hard for her to make new friends.

Although it took only a moment to realize these weren't the kind of guys any level-headed woman wanted to be friends with.

I couldn't hear their conversation from the inside of my truck, but the short guy placed his hand on Ruby's forearm in a tight grip. Her face was covered in fear as she took a few steps back in an effort to get away. The tall guy was smiling and enjoying his friend's assault.

When she tried to shake him off and he gripped her tighter, moving so close their noses were nearly touching, I opened the truck door.

I don't fucking think so.

Ruby might have been a gutsy city girl, but she was no match for two guys who had her backed into the doorway of an abandoned business. And I could see from her wide eyes and deadly white face, she was well aware of that.

In about four long strides, I was across the street. I started by getting my hands on the short guy, the one holding Ruby, grabbing him by the scruff of the neck.

"Let her go," I growled.

He looked over his shoulder and with his free arm, tried to reach me. But I had a good sixty pounds and several inches on him, and even more important, I was fucking pissed.

His buddy, eager to help out his friend, took two steps toward me, walking right into the punch I laid on his upper breastbone. He staggered backward before he fell, the wind knocked out of him.

"Roman, watch it!" Ruby screamed as I turned back to her, now free of the short guy's grip.

Thanks to her warning, I dodged his swing, catching his arm on the follow through. I bent it up behind his back until he screamed and fell to his knees in pain. Confident neither of them was getting up off the ground anytime soon, I pulled Ruby to me and against my chest, holding her and hoping to calm her shaking.

"Let's get out of here."

But before we left, I turned to the losers writhing on the ground. "If either of you do that to a woman again, I'll make sure it's the last time you do it. Do you understand?" I hissed.

To my delight, Ruby broke out of my arms and ran back towards them, landing a blow right to the crotch of the short one who'd grabbed her, with the toe of her boot.

Holy shit. Every man's worst nightmare.

And fucking good for her. Damn.

They groaned over their injuries, the one with the smashed balls coughing and spitting. I walked Ruby back to the truck, where I helped her get in and buckled her seatbelt for her.

"Oh my god. I don't know what I would have done if you hadn't come along. I was tucked into the doorway of that closed business. I was so afraid, I couldn't even scream."

Fuckers.

"I'm sorry that happened, Ruby." I reached across the seat and took her hand, which was cold and still trembling. "I'll kill those bastards if they ever try anything like that again."

"Should we call the—"

But she stopped. She'd grown up in ranch country and knew we solved our problems ourselves. The cops were only ever a last resort and were usually less effective than our innate scrappiness. Hell, that's why she'd kicked the shit out of that one guy.

"I don't think anyone in New York would have done that for me."

I glanced at her pale face. "I find that hard to believe. Especially for a girl as pretty as you."

She smiled slightly and looked out her side window to hide her face. But before she did, I caught the blush rising up her cheeks.

A modest woman. I liked that.

16

ROMAN

WHEN WE PULLED UP IN FRONT OF THE HOUSE, I POPPED out to help her to the door. "I'll get one of the guys to bring the truck home later. We need you to take it easy. Get some rest."

She held out her hand as she stepped down from the truck, and didn't let go of it even after we'd entered the house. In fact, she headed for the stairs, leading me behind her.

Well then.

When we got to her room, she turned to me. "Will you come in? Just for a bit?"

I pushed her bedroom closed behind us.

Without giving anything much thought, I hoisted Ruby until her legs wrapped around my waist, and brought her over to a small writing desk in the corner of her room. I set her down and wove my fingers through her hair, taking in every inch of her beautiful face.

She reached toward me for a kiss, but I pulled back just far enough to stop her. I wasn't done drinking her in.

"Just let me look at you."

Her lips parted slightly and her eyelids got heavy as my words calmed her. That's when I brought my lips to her temple, touching her with them, then moving on to another spot on her face. I had to kiss every inch of her like I'd wanted to do since she'd arrived. I was like a starving man who'd finally found food. If I didn't satisfy my hunger, I wasn't sure what I'd do.

I brushed my lips over her eyes and then her nose, finally reaching her mouth, which I hovered above, feeling her warm breath mingle with mine. I took hold of her chin, and when I pressed my mouth to hers, she emitted a small moan. If my cock wasn't hard already, it sure as hell was now.

The interrupted kiss we'd shared in the foyer a few nights previous had been quick. Almost chaste. But this was the kiss of two people who needed something wild and uncontrolled.

Still seated on the desk, Ruby reached for my belt and had my jeans open in moments. Her hand slipped into my boxers, and when she found my cock, it was all I could do not to explode right there.

Get a grip, asshole.

I pushed into her, pumping her grip, which slid from my balls to head and back.

"Fuck…"

I pulled her T-shirt off, followed by her bra, and pushed her delicious tits together so I could enjoy them both at once. My rough thumbs ran over her nipples and when I pulled on them, she dropped her head and gasped.

Placing my hands under her ass, I picked her up again and brought her to the bed, shimmying her jeans and panties to her ankles, only slowed by the boots and socks I needed to toss aside.

And then my girl was naked.

Fuck if she wasn't beautiful. I kissed her smooth, flat stomach, my tongue traveling lower until I reached the small landing strip of hair above her pussy. With my gaze fixed to hers, I parted her legs slowly, until I could feel the heat pouring off her and breathe her sweet scent. Still not taking my eyes off hers, I ran my fingers through her wet slit, drawing them to my mouth for a taste.

She spread her legs further for me.

"Good girl."

I finally broke our gaze and turned to the pussy I'd been tasting. I gently opened her lips so I could see her most private parts, and with one more glance at her beautiful eyes, I buried my face between her thighs, lapping her from ass to clit, only stopping at her opening to see how deep I could go with my tongue.

Writhing under me, Ruby's hands flew to her face like she didn't know what to do. The more I licked her, the more she rocked her hips, arching and twisting, her moans growing louder.

"Baby, I need to fuck you." Somewhere along the line, my voice had gone hoarse.

She nodded. "Yes, you do."

I drew my own T-shirt over my head, then got to my feet to kick off my boots and jeans. But before I chucked my pants aside, I reached into my wallet for a condom.

I crawled back between Ruby's creamy thighs, and found her hand on her clit, making small circles.

I fucking loved seeing a woman play with herself.

As I watched the pretty sight, I sheathed myself and got into position at her opening. "Guide me in when you're ready, darlin'," I growled.

She reached down and ran my cock through her slick folds, spreading her cream and teasing me to the point of craziness.

"You're so fucking beautiful, baby," I whispered, pushing inside her.

She gasped as she stretched to accommodate me, her pussy milking my cock to the point where I had to stop so I didn't immediately blow my load.

"God, Roman," she sighed, running her open palms over her nipples, her head arched back and her eyes closed.

"Give it to me. I want it hard. I need it hard."

Holy fuck. Was she kidding?

"I promise, baby. I'm gonna fuck the shit out of you."

I slid in and out until I was sure she was ready and then pistoned her pussy, picking up speed until I pounded so hard my balls slapped her ass.

"Oh god, I'm coming, Roman," she cried. "Yes, yes, yes…"

I held back as long as I could. I didn't remember sex ever having been like this, so unselfconsciously sensual and raw. Ruby's chest flushed pink, and she gasped for air. My last drive into her was when she whispered, "Kiss me. Kiss me, please."

I was a goner, exploding inside my beauty, pulling my lips from hers to watch her face twist as one orgasm after another careened through her.

She was so fucking responsive and beautiful, soft in the right places and taut in others.

"Fuck…" I bellowed, pushing myself deep inside her one last time, spurting until I was panting and dizzy.

I ditched the condom and fell beside her, wrapping her in my arms and legs. In moments she was making soft girl snores, her fingers tangled in my hair like she'd never let go.

17

RUBY

JUST LIKE ROMAN HAD PROMISED, MY TRUCK—OR THE
truck he was letting me borrow—was out front when I
got up the next morning. I wasn't sure who brought it
back from town after my big scare, or how the guys
worked it out, but I guess it didn't matter. They just took
care of business.

Someone bothers me?

Roman beats the shit out of them.

I leave my truck somewhere?

They go get it and bring it home.

This was one of the things about life in the west I'd
nearly forgotten. Instead of bitching and moaning when
things didn't go right, people here just made them work.

Took matters into their own hands. There was little choice. You did what you had to do.

Whereas in New York, none of the guys I knew would have come to my rescue like Roman had. They'd have called the cops, for sure. Even hollered for help. But they never would have risked getting hit, even if I were being dragged down the street by my freaking hair.

Roman.

The man kept his promises.

Especially the one where he'd promised to fuck me hard. And damn if I wasn't feeling it now. Not that I was complaining. Oh hell no.

I needed what he gave me, big time. It was an escape, to lose myself in his furious lovemaking. Something about us both had been almost desperate to feed the attraction we'd had to each other since I'd arrived at Flood Creek.

He hadn't let me stay at the house just because he was a nice guy—although he certainly was. He'd seen the way I'd looked at him in the midst of my confusion about my parents taking off. They might have been my number one concern at the time, but the handsome silver fox in front of me was a close second. And he wasn't in second place for long.

Regardless, I couldn't stay at Flood Creek forever. It was now home to different people, who had their own plans for it. I didn't want to hold them back by expecting things to stay as they'd always been. I couldn't let myself get too comfortable.

Without any family here, why would I stay in Flood

Creek, anyway? I wasn't about to deliver flowers every morning for the rest of my life.

But I couldn't go back to New York, either. As much as Posey was begging me via her daily texts, I'd crashed and burned in that town. It just wasn't my kind of place. I didn't understand the nuances of workplace chitchat, or managing the people around me. I always said the wrong thing, which delighted my sadistic boss, Sylvie, because I was just feeding her more ammo to treat me like shit with.

The last straw had been when she'd asked me to inflate the hours we'd worked for one of our clients. I'd questioned it because it was, well, dishonest. But apparently Sylvie had been pressured to increase billable hours. Because I didn't just do as she'd asked without question, she'd screamed at me in front of the entire office.

It was funny. She'd screamed at me before. Hell, she'd screamed at everyone. But this time, while she was going off on me, I looked out the window into the office building across the street. Were there better jobs out there, at least for me? And I spotted someone who looked like he was being berated just like I was. But instead of disengaging like I had, and closing his ears to the barrage of insults being hurled at him, he wore the expression of humiliation and pain that I knew so well.

I was done. Just done.

In a daze and without even thinking, I told Sylvie to go fuck herself in a quiet, flat voice, as if someone else were saying the words. And before I could even get them all the way out, she'd responded that I was fired.

And that was that.

With a sense of relief, if not amazement that I'd sort-of stood up to Sylvie, I slipped my trench coat on, dropped my coffee mug into my Kate Spade tote, and left.

Instead of taking the subway, I walked all the way home with a smile on my face and the city's grimy breeze whipping my hair. I was free. I was happy. It was fucking great.

Posey told me later that everyone thought I was the biggest badass in the world for giving Sylvie the figurative middle finger. That after I'd left, she'd stood there with her mouth open, confused by my defiance. Then, she'd returned to her office, slammed the door, and closed the blinds.

I didn't feel much when Posey told me this. No smugness, no satisfaction, no delight. I just knew I could not look back.

Had I let my psycho boss ruin New York for me? Perhaps. But I paid the next month's rent to my roommate, packed my things in a rental car, and hit the road. It was like I had tunnel vision, and the first road out of New York was all I could see. Sticking around was no longer an option. New York was over. A blip on the screen. And rapidly becoming part of my past.

So my claim that I was back in Flood Creek for nothing more than a 'visit' was obviously bullshit. It wouldn't be long before people would start figuring that out, if they hadn't already. And because I no longer had a home here, I'd have to eventually hit the road again. Not sure where I'd go, but I'd have to leave.

I had to. There was no choice. After all, I'd just banged Jameson and Roman, and had a serious make-out session with Cam. And I had no plans to stop. Fuck them if they didn't like it. As long as I was here, I was treating myself to a little fun.

Before I got into my truck to head over to Melanie's —a dinner invitation I'd wanted to avoid but just couldn't—I saw one of the ranch hands watching me from a distance.

What was that guy's name again?

I waved. "Hey," I called.

He just stood there looking at me.

"How're you doing today?" I asked.

He abruptly turned and walked away. Really fast.

Roley was his name. Roley.

What a weirdo. Actually, a lot of ranch hands were weirdos. Or should I say they were just unusual? Many were drifters who lived their lives differently from the rest of us. But it was all good. Ranches needed people like that guy for what they could do, not for their sparkling personalities.

18

RUBY

Since the day I'd run into Melanie, when she'd offered me both hairstyle and fashion advice, she'd hounded me to come for dinner with her family. I'd avoided committing, not because I didn't want to see her —although I imagined her house to be pure chaos, which was beyond stress inducing for someone who hadn't been around kids much—but because I wasn't ready to answer the litany of questions I knew would come my way. She'd want to know *everything*, and I didn't even know what *everything* entailed yet.

"Oh my gosh," she exclaimed when I arrived, thrusting at her a large bouquet of flowers I'd gotten for free from my boss. She sniffed them deeply. "Heaven. Just like heaven. C'mon in, honey," she sang.

My dear Melanie. In spite of my selfish misgivings, the moment I heard her voice I was happy I'd come. The woman was a force of nature and comforting at the same time. I was lucky to have her on my team.

Or was I on her team?

She draped an arm around my shoulders and directed me through the living room, where we goose-stepped a landmine of toys and other kid stuff until we reached what she called the 'playroom.' There, the three older kids were screaming and throwing shit at each other and didn't stop until Melanie hollared at them to.

The room went silent, and all I could hear was her baby, sitting in a highchair in the kitchen, gurgling and cooing.

"Kids, I want you to say hello to my best friend from childhood, Ruby Lee Whitaker."

They stared at me for a moment, then looked back at their mother. They could clearly not give a shit about me and wasn't sure what their mother wanted them to do.

Guess they didn't get visitors much.

"Can you say hello to my friend," she asked in a sugary voice.

Three mumbled *hellos* came my way.

I waved. "Hi."

"Now, Mommy and Ruby Lee are going to be in the kitchen while I finish dinner, so I do not want any screaming. And JoJo," she said, pointing at the biggest, "come here and feed the baby."

JoJo didn't like the sound of that. "Momma, I don't want—"

But Melanie held one finger up, and the whining came to an abrupt stop.

Wow. She had this shit down.

She glanced at me and gestured toward the kitchen, where we headed.

I helped myself to a stool at the counter, and Melanie set two wine glasses and a bottle of red in front of me.

"I'll let you do the honors, Ruby Lee."

"When'd you start drinking wine, Melanie?" I asked.

She took the glass I poured for her and lowered her voice when JoJo entered the kitchen. "Soon as I started having kids. I love them to death, but sometimes the only way to get through the day is with a glass of wine. Or two." She cackled just like she did when we were in high school with the kind of laugh that, if it didn't annoy the shit out of you, would make you smile.

While she blathered on about happenings in Flood Creek and the surrounding towns, I realized I missed her. Not that she ever would have come with me, but she probably would have handled New York far better than I did. She was just generally tougher—more kickass—and probably a lot smarter when it came down to it.

She was the one who should have gone to college. She was the one who should have tried her hand at a career in New York. Not me.

But what would I have done? Stayed behind and married my high school sweetheart, Jameson? That would have made a lot of people happy, including my parents and his mother.

Not sure it would have worked for me, though.

She turned back to me after she'd handed JoJo a bottle for the baby.

"You have a good little helper," I said.

Melanie took a swig of her wine and raised her eyebrows. "You'd damn well better believe I do. No one lives in this house for free, is what I say. As soon as you're old enough, you get a chore or two. You should see my four-year-old with the Dustbuster after dinner every night. He's a champ at getting all the food the kids have dropped on the floor."

I looked around the kitchen, every surface covered with stuff—papers, toys, appliances, dishes. It would drive me crazy. But Melanie was unfazed, just like she was about most things.

She leaned on the counter toward me. "Okay, before Hank gets home, tell me. Do you think you and Jameson will get back together?"

And, there it was.

"Oh my god, no, Melanie. He hates my guts."

After our blowout of last week, I could say that with confidence.

She smiled coyly, like she knew more than I did. Which was entirely possible. Her ability to read situations had always been better than mine. "Then why'd you come back?" she asked in a singsong voice.

Shit. I wasn't ready to share the whole sorry tale about work.

So I shrugged. "Well, I thought I'd come back to see my parents and surprise them. But... we all know how that turned out."

She shimmied her shoulders. "C'mon. You weren't even a little curious about Jameson?"

Jesus, she was persistent.

"Melanie, he hates my freaking guts. I mean, I wish him well, but he doesn't want anything to do with me. Take my word for it."

I decided to change the subject. Well, *try* to change the subject. "I wish you could have visited me in New York. It was a lot of fun. Pretty wild."

I started telling her about my job and friends there, but it soon became apparent she wasn't nearly as interested in that as she was in my love life. It occurred to me that as hard as I tried to get out of Flood Creek and prove myself somewhere else, I was the only one it mattered to. Life in New York was meaningless around here. No one was all that interested in hearing my stories. They listened to be polite—up to a point. Then their eyes glazed over.

Probably just as well since I didn't exactly have a happy ending to share, anyway.

Melanie's baby started to fuss, and when she picked him up out of the highchair his older sister ran back to the playroom. The sounds coming from there started to get louder, involving screams and things hitting the walls.

And just then, Hank came in, roaring through the door with more force than his rambunctious family could muster all together.

Jesus. What a place.

It was crazy, dramatic, and cozy, reminding me of a

big, warm hand closing around you, letting you know you were safe, and loved.

That's how it had been with my family.

I excused myself for the bathroom, hoping to get there before the growing lump in my throat turned to tears. Shit, I don't think I'd cried as much in the last couple weeks as I had in the last year of my life.

After stepping on a couple squeaky bath toys, I sat on the closed toilet lid and put my head in my hands. What the hell was I doing? I'd bailed on New York, messed around with all the guys at the ranch, and lied my ass off about nearly everything going on in my life.

Were things better or worse here than they'd been in New York? It was debatable. If nothing else, they were different. And not entirely comfortable. But I was making it work. Right? I had to give myself credit for that.

I splashed water on my face, finger combed my hair, and went out to face Melanie and her wild menagerie.

PLAIN AND SIMPLE, Melanie spun through life like a cyclone, and I had mad respect for her. When I was finally ready to leave her house at midnight, she was still going strong, gabbing away, drinking wine, and occasionally yelling at one of her kids who'd gotten out of bed or committed some other offense. Her competency and multitasking would have put anyone in the corporate world to shame.

When I got home, I slipped into the house and because it was so late, I removed my boots to tiptoe over the hardwood floors. At the top of the stairs, I turned in the direction of my room but stopped.

What was that noise?

I crept by the room that had been my brother's growing up, and which was now Cam's. I stood outside, silently.

Heavy breathing accompanied by the occasional grunt seeped into the hallway from the other side of the door.

Who was Cam with?

But as I listened longer, all tingly and hot, I realized he was alone.

And jerking off.

I put my hand on the doorknob without thinking. Actually, I was purposely not thinking because if I'd stopped to do that, I'd chicken out and run right back to my own room. I pushed the door open slightly and leaned into the opening.

"Cam?" I whispered into the dark room.

The noises came to a complete stop.

Ugh. I hadn't wanted to ruin his fun.

"Ruby, what do you want?" he hissed through the dark.

I stepped inside and pushed the door closed, leaning up against it. "I... I heard you, Cam. Just now. When I came home."

He sighed. "Sorry about that. You can go to bed now."

"I don't want to."

I wished I could see him in the dim light, but he was probably glad I couldn't. I hoped he wasn't too embarrassed, but if he were, I was going to make him forget any of that damn fast.

"What do you want then?" he asked, his voice softer.

"I want to help you finish the job you started."

Had I really just said that?

There was silence for a moment, then he cleared his throat. "Come here."

I set down my boots and purse and slowly walked toward Cam, shuffling my feet to avoid the clothes all over his floor. I knew I'd reached the bed when my knee bounced off the edge of it.

Cam's hand found me, and ran up the side of my hip. "Take your clothes off," he demanded.

Damn.

So, I did and crawled into bed next to him. His sheets were warm and smelled of fresh laundry, and when he moved to cover me with his body, his own scent was even more delicious—a combination of simple soap and the great outdoors.

He hovered above me. "Can I tell you something, Ruby?"

"Sure." I ran my hands down his strong back and over his rock-hard butt cheeks.

"I've always wanted you. I have. But someone else always got to you first. Well that, and your brother would have killed me."

I put my hands on either side of his face and lifted my

lips to his. "Thank you. That's the sweetest thing I think I've ever heard."

His mouth crashed into mine with years of wanting, and I returned his passion to make up for lost time.

As one of my brother's friends, Cam had always been off limits. But he was the only one in that guy posse who ever gave me the time of day. When Bud's friends had descended on the house when we were kids, they pretty much ignored me. But Cam always stopped by my room to say hello.

During his senior year—my sophomore year—he'd gotten his girlfriend pregnant. That had unleashed a shit storm of drama, especially when the girl moved away and he didn't follow. I'd always wondered if there was more to the story than was shared, but it wasn't my business then. Would it be now?

But first things first.

I reached down between the two of us and wrapped my fingers around Cam's stiff cock. I ran my fingers up the soft skin of his shaft, and over the bulbous head where precum had gathered.

With my other hand, I cupped his balls. His breathing returned to the gritty sound I'd heard earlier, and when I rubbed the flat of my palm over the head of his cock, he groaned again.

He pumped his hips, fucking my hand, until he let out a growl and shuddered. His warm cum shot all over my stomach, and his head dropped into the nook of my shoulder.

"Fuck," he said, falling onto his back. He reached for some tissues next to his bed and cleaned me up.

"Hey, Cam, can I ask you a question?"

"Of course."

"How come you didn't marry that girl in high school, the one you got pregnant?"

At the time, it was quite the scandal, and I always thought it was a little dishonorable of him to not own up to his responsibility.

"It got complicated. There are things you don't know. Things no one knows."

I'd gathered as much. Things were rarely as they seemed.

19

———

JAMESON

"I've been thinking, guys. I don't believe it's a good idea to have Ruby around."

I hated to be a dick, but I wasn't going to keep my mouth shut about this.

Roman put his head in his hand and rubbed his forehead. I knew he wasn't going to like what I had to say. But we were business partners, and I was looking out for what was best for the ranch.

Well, and for myself. If I were to be truthful about it.

I suppose I could be more high-minded. Just forget about our past, and especially the blow up we'd had the week before. But I just couldn't see anything good coming from having someone like Ruby around the ranch. She'd had her chance to make a life here and when she didn't want to, her father sold to the guys and me.

She no longer belonged here.

She belonged back in New York with the preppy east coasters who couldn't do a hard day's work if their lives depended on it. I could just see one of those suited-up douchebag Wall Street types trying to move a bale of hay or wrangle a horse. They'd fucking run home crying.

Ruby had been away from Flood Ranch for a long time. This wasn't her scene anymore.

If it ever had been.

She might have known how to clean horse stalls when she was growing up, but I bet if she had to do it now, she'd have a damn heart attack.

So I really wanted to get Roman and Cam on the same page as me and agree Ruby's visit here had a time limit on it. Regardless of how gorgeous and sexy she was. And how much we all craved her.

I was past that now. I didn't want anything to do with her.

Most of the time.

I'd avoided her like the plague since the day we'd quarreled. It hadn't been easy to keep my distance since the ranch was both my home and place of work now. But I'd managed.

'Course she'd worked to avoid me too.

Cam set down his coffee. "Jameson, I know you have a beef with Ruby going way back, but you have to move on from that. We all have shit from our past that eats at us. You're no different from anyone else."

Roman sighed. "I have to agree with Cam. I don't see a downside to having her here. She's friendly, easy going, nice to look at, doesn't bother anybody—"

"What?" I interrupted. "She's a high maintenance pain in the ass. I say she needs to go, and soon," I said, louder than I meant to.

"*Well, good morning to you too.*"

Our heads whipped in the direction of the sharp female voice calling out from the kitchen doorway.

Shit.

Ruby. Of course.

Head down and eyes narrowed like a pissed off bull, she stormed toward us where we were seated in the breakfast nook, hands on hips, lips pursed.

After giving us each, individually, her death stare, she spoke. "I'll have you guys know I don't plan to stay here any longer than I absolutely have to. So don't think you're doing me some big fucking favor. I know I have no claim to anything in this house, even though I grew up in it. So don't worry. I have no plans to stick around, if for no other reason than I wouldn't give you creeps the satisfaction."

Roman reached for her hand, but she snapped it back.

Was he really going to poke that hornet's nest?

Cam put his hands up like a *stop* sign. "Now, Ruby, Jameson doesn't speak for us all. So please calm down. But hey, aren't you just here for a visit, anyway? You're going back to New York, eventually, right?"

Ruby's face turned red and she sputtered.

"Don't tell me to calm down. And New York has nothing to do with this."

Um. Okay.

I didn't want her to be mad at Cam and Roman since I was the one who'd brought the whole thing up. "Look, Ruby—"

"Fuck off," she spat, and stormed through the house and out the front door.

Roman sighed and Cam gave me the stink eye. "Nice work, buddy. Now she's pissed at all of us."

Mary, over in the kitchen, slammed a couple pans around to make her feelings known.

"Damn, Jameson," Roman said, shaking his head, "you really stepped into it."

Fuck. I hadn't figured she'd hear me. I didn't even think she was home. Her truck—well, the ranch's truck—hadn't been out front when I drove up to the main house that morning.

"Dude, I think you'd better go after her. Talk to her," Cam said.

Oh, hell.

I took one more swig of coffee and jogged toward the door.

20

JAMESON

BY THE TIME I CAUGHT UP TO RUBY, I WAS SWEATY AND
out of breath. It seemed, among other things, that one of
the habits she'd picked up in New York was speed walking. When I got outside and saw her heading down the
ranch road, she was all elbows and ass.

"Yo, Ruby. Hold up," I called.

She just walked faster.

Cripes, how did she do that?

I grabbed her arm, which pulled her to a screeching
stop. I knew I was taking my chances doing it, and that I
could end up with a black eye, but I had to get her to
listen.

She whipped around, her face streaked with tears.

And I felt like the world's biggest asshole. What was

wrong with me? Cam and Roman were right. She wasn't bothering anyone.

Except my fucking pride.

"I'm sorry, Ruby. I was mouthing off like an idiot. I don't want you to go."

While running after her, I'd planned to force myself to say those words. But now that they'd passed through my lips, I realized they were true. I didn't have to force myself at all.

I didn't want her to go. I'd just been acting like a dick.

"My pride was hurt, Ruby. And that's what was behind my unkind words. I'm sorry."

And as if I hadn't said anything, and as if I weren't even there, she looked around, across the land she'd grown up on.

Her voice was almost dreamy. "Nothing here is mine anymore. It used to be. At least that's how I felt when I was growing up. I could do anything on this land I wanted to. And now I shouldn't really even be here."

She gazed dreamily across the valley to the mountains in the distance, shaking her head. "But what did I expect, after being gone for so long? Of course my parents were free to do whatever they wanted with the place. I had no claim on it. And neither did my brother."

I'd been dying to tell her about our plans for the ranch since I'd first seen her. But our quarrel had gotten in the way. Maybe now was the time.

"Ruby, I'd like to show you what we're doing here with the ranch. It might not be yours anymore, but you'll be pleased. I'd like to think we'll make you proud. We all love the ranch and plan to treat it with utmost respect."

Her face softened. "I'd like that."

We walked back to the house and got in my truck, driving in silence until we reached the old bunkhouses.

"Oh my god. These places are such dumps." She wrinkled her nose.

"Not anymore. When I told you I lived in one of the bunkhouses, I didn't have the chance to tell you how we'd fixed them up."

She got down out of the truck and walked toward the building that, when she'd last been there, had been a shitty old dump shared by cowboys and wranglers. It was now divided up into individual suites, each with its own entrance, and decorated in what my mother liked to call *western ranch chic*, with exposed log beams, vintage cowboy paraphernalia on the walls, huge stone fireplaces, and hand-sewn quilts.

"C'mon. This one is mine." I pushed my door open and stepped aside for her to enter.

I was proud of my place, I couldn't lie. Hell, I was proud of all the work we'd done on the ranch in the short time we'd owned it, but none more than having turned a rustic old bunkhouse into accommodations that people from all over the world would stay in to get a taste of life on a ranch.

Planning board permitting, of course.

"*No way.*" She turned slowly, taking it all in.

While I bent to light a fire, she ran her hand over the

crackly leather of the chairs facing the fireplace, her gaze settling on a painting just above the mantle.

Her voice caught. "Did my *mother* paint that?"

I stood back, admiring the growing fire and the beautiful painting above it. "Yup. It's one of hers. I remember her oil painting from when we were growing up. She never gave it up. In fact, she gave us paintings for all the rooms."

Ruby put a hand over her trembling mouth. "What do you mean, all the rooms?"

"The bunkhouse is all suites now, decorated just like mine. The idea is to keep Flood Creek a working ranch, but also a small resort where people can come and experience ranch life. We have ten rooms like this now and plan to add more."

She looked at me, her eyes wide. "Did my parents know your plans?"

I took a seat near the fire and gestured for her to do the same.

"They sure did. Is that making you sad?"

She shrugged. "Not sure. It's just so weird to see one of my mom's paintings up there. But it's also comforting. Like she's close by."

I was beginning to realize how hard all this had been for Ruby, and how many regrets she was probably juggling at that moment.

"Your parents were really excited for us to develop the ranch into something more than it was. I don't think they would have sold it to us, otherwise. I suspect they'll be back here at some point, possibly as tenants, or maybe even as managers of the resort."

Ruby lowered herself to her seat and hung her head, a curtain of hair swinging in the way of her pretty face.

"Are you going to have guests anytime soon?"

I reached over the small table separating our chairs and took her hand. After the way I'd acted earlier, I was frankly surprised she let me. But in her state of over-whelm, I was hoping she'd forgotten, at least temporarily, what a dick I'd been.

"Things have gotten… complicated. Turns out the planning board is hesitating to give us the permits we need."

She frowned. "Why?"

"Most likely for a couple reasons. First, I don't think they see how it will benefit the town overall. You know, people are generally resistant to change. And second, it seems like there is some bad blood behind the board and Roman, dating back to when he went to them years ago about the issue with your father."

She shook her head. "Ugh. I hope it gets worked out. It is strange to think of Flood Creek Ranch hosting guests. I like the idea, though. It's bold."

Exactly. I knew she'd get it.

I jumped to my feet, excited as I always was about the project. "You know how many people would love to see a working ranch up close? Maybe ride horses, deliver a baby pig or cow, or learn how we herd bison?"

Her face exploded into a smile. "Oh my god, totally. It sounds like summer camp for grown ups."

That made me laugh.

She slapped her hand on the arm of her chair. "When I was in New York, people were insanely curious when I told them I'd grown up on a ranch. Every single one of my friends begged me to take them home with me. You're on to something. I know it."

I was so happy she shared our vision that I pulled her out of her chair and kissed her.

And almost as quickly, I let her go. "Oh shit. Sorry. I got carried away."

Her lips were pink from my hard kiss. "No, you didn't. You *wanted* to kiss me. Just like I wanted you to."

She knew me too well.

Taking her by the hand, I led her to my bed, where I put my hands on either side of her beautiful face, and kissed her impatiently.

Pulling back, she gazed at me, running a finger over my brow, down my cheek, and along my jawline. Her touch was soft but fiery at the same time, and while she might have been melancholy moments before, she now radiated a desire that was driving me fucking senseless.

I pulled her sweater over her head and reached to unhook her bra. Then I lay her back and with one thigh between her legs, pressed her breasts together until each nipple was pink and swollen from my rough attentions.

"God, Jameson, that feels so nice," she murmured, arching her back to grind her sex against my thigh.

I abandoned her tits and turned to her jeans, which I opened and pulled down her hips until I was stopped by her high-heeled boots. I got them out of the way and soon had her lying there nearly naked.

"So beautiful," I whispered, running my lips across her abdomen. My fingers found the heat between her legs and I massaged her through her silky panties.

Cupping her sex, I pressed my palm into her, providing just enough pressure to tease, but not enough to offer any sort of satisfaction.

Yet.

She fumbled with my buttons, pushing my shirt off, and moved to my belt and fly until she could reach inside my jeans, wrapping her fingers around my erection. I moved my hips just enough to fuck her hand, realizing that if I weren't inside her soon I'd be wasting my hard-on instead of pleasing her with it.

I got to my feet and kicked off my boots and jeans, reaching into my nightstand for a condom. Sheathing myself, I crawled back between her legs.

"I'm going to fuck you with every inch of my dick. I want you to feel me inside you, stretching you, and filling you so I can make you come hard and loud."

She looked back at me, her eyelids heavy and her smile slight. "Exactly what I want."

I grabbed her panties and with a hard yank, tore them off and tossed them aside. I positioned myself near her opening, and running a finger through her slit, found it wet, her pussy lips puffy with anticipation.

With one hand on each breast, I kneed her legs apart and inched inside her, pausing when she gasped.

"God, you're big," she groaned, but nevertheless put her hands on my hips and pulled me closer.

"Are you okay?" I asked when I was nearly all the way in.

She nodded, her breath now raspy. "Your cock is amazing. I want you to fuck me with it until I scream."

Well shit, she didn't need to ask twice.

I pistoned her slowly at first to make sure she was nice and wet and then faster, driving into her pussy while she milked my dick with her pussy contractions.

I struggled to hold my cum so I could feel and hear her explode one more time. I didn't want her burning passion to quiet, ever, and found myself wishing the moment could last.

But there would be other times like this, I hoped, and with my balls drawing up tight, I exploded into my girl as we finished in a perfect rhythm.

"Fuck, baby," I bellowed with one last thrust.

She joined me in another orgasm, both of us shaking, and me wondering how the hell we'd gone so long without each other.

21

RUBY

NOW *THAT*, I HADN'T BEEN EXPECTING.

The conversation I'd heard among the guys in the kitchen devastated me. I suppose that's why I blew up like I did. And even if it were true that only Jameson was behind it, something about it bit me to the core. I was already walking around Flood Creek with so much uncertainty and the doubt, I didn't need another blow. And boy did I light into Jameson.

But hey, I was nothing if not resilient.

When it came down to it, what fucking choice did I have?

I might have felt like rolling myself into a little ball every now and then and just blowing away like tumble-weed, but that's not how life worked. The only real option was to hold your head up and get on with it. Something, somehow, someday would work out in your favor. It always did. Well, nearly always.

Like Jameson coming after me with an apology. The man had hated me, I was sure of it. I never expected any remorse on his side. And yet when he realized how hurt I was, it seemed like he had a change of heart. I had to give him credit for that.

Most people didn't have the balls to own up to their shit.

And from time to time, I was one of them. I could learn from him.

Now, I was lying in his bed, in the remarkable renovation of the crummy old bunkhouse where my parents had housed itinerants and drifters over the years when they'd required seasonal workers.

Of course, when I was growing up, I was forbidden to go anywhere near the bunkhouse. It was not a place for the owner's daughter to hang out or even visit. But I had peeked in once or twice when I had reinforcements like Melanie around. We weren't quite sure what we were supposed to be afraid of, and still weren't after our spying sessions, but it was fascinating to see a group of rough and ready-type men trying to live together under one roof. Even the kitchen was in the room where they slept.

It was so different from the pretty, feminine bedrooms we had to ourselves that no siblings were allowed to enter without permission. The bunkhouse was gross in our estimation, but an endlessly fascinating illustration of raw masculinity with its tobacco-chewing, rough-talking, wiry ranch workers. It was no wonder Melanie had married Hank, who had worked so hard he was now foreman of the ranch where he'd been employed since high school.

Cowboys were fucking hot. There was just no way around it.

Jameson stirred as my thoughts raced, marveling at how he'd created a cozy little home that looked like something out of a Ralph Lauren catalogue. In the dim light of the sunrise, I could make out an incredible deer antler chandelier hanging high from a beam that just pulled the whole room together.

How had he pulled this off? Was my mom the decorating brain behind it all?

Once again, I found myself wondering why I was the last one to learn this shit. But I had to get over that. I was catching up, even if was it occasionally painful.

I was dying for the bathroom, but Jameson's arms were wrapped around me so tightly I didn't have the heart to move. Plus, it had been so long since anyone had made me feel so cherished, I wanted to draw the moment out for as long as possible.

After all, I wasn't going to be on the ranch forever. I might as well enjoy myself while I could.

Right? I couldn't possibly stick around, even though Jameson had apologized for griping about my presence. I had no business there, and besides, I couldn't make a long-term living delivering flowers every morning. No matter how many freebies I got.

Jameson shifted, snoring a little, and his hand brushed across my breasts. My nipples jumped to attention and there was a clenching between my legs, as if to say *hey, how about some more?*

Well, damn.

I arched to press my ass against him, and found that his cock was fully hard, even as he slept soundly.

Seemed like it was time to wake the man up.

I eased out of his embrace and crawled under the covers, nudging him onto his back. He grunted quietly and his erection popped up next to my face. Making a tent under the covers, I slowly ran my tongue along his length and felt him twitch under my touch.

I had to admit, I was giddy at the idea of waking him up this way, something I'd never done with any guy. I'd never liked anyone enough to want to suck his dick without the promise of anything else right behind it, if I were honest with myself. It seemed like the guys in New York went through the motions of oral sex not so much because they liked it but because it was part of the process of getting laid.

While I couldn't see his expression, the coarseness of the next groan he emitted let me know my attentions were bringing him back to the land of the living, and when his hand found my head and his fingers ran through my hair, I knew I'd aroused him in more than one way.

"*Ruby,*" he murmured.

The sound of him breathing my name drove me, and I

wrapped my lips around his swelling erection, tonguing and swallowing the warm precum seeping from his cock.

He opened his legs further, and grabbed my hair harder. And yet, none of it was rough or demanding. Or intimidating. I wanted to be there, with Jameson, making him feel good before he started his day.

He bucked his hips to fuck my mouth, my brow growing sweaty from the heat coming off him trapped by the tented blankets. As if he could read my mind, he swept the covers back and our gazes met, me with my mouth full and eyes slightly watering, he with a grinding jaw. The cooler morning air was a relief on my skin, and the look on his face emboldened me to take him even more deeply.

Arching his back, he pounded a fist on the bed when he bounced against the back of my throat. I gagged. I'll admit it.

"Goddamn," he hollered, arching one more time to drive himself in my mouth as deeply as possible. "Suck me, beautiful, suck my cock…"

With one hand still on my head, he ran the fingers of the other around my stretched lips to feel my effort. I gripped his strong thighs for purchase and looked up as his neck strained, revealing corded muscles. In relief, he called my name one more time.

My mouth flooded with cum and I swallowed what I could, milking what was left using my hands, aiming it on my breasts, which were quickly covered in his seed.

He pulled me to him, holding me tight while he shuddered, his body soaked with sweat that smelled so good I pushed my face into his chest to inhale more.

22

RUBY

WHILE I DROVE TO THE FLORIST THAT MORNING TO SEE what deliveries I had, I called my brother. We'd never been particularly close and were even less so now, years after we'd both left town. But I was dying to know if he knew about Mom and Dad's decision to sell the ranch and hit the road, or whether I was going to be the first to spring it on him.

Why keep the surprise all to myself?

But it turned out that, once again, I was the only one ill-informed. Or non-informed.

"Buddy."

He grunted and yawned. He was in a time zone an hour earlier than mine. Maybe I shouldn't have called him at eight a.m., but hell, he had to get up some time.

"Ruby Lee?" he asked, clearing the sleep out of his voice.

He was never going to call me by my preferred name, no matter how many times I'd asked. So, I'd given up.

But then, he preferred Bud to Buddy, which I refused to adopt until he accommodated me. I could be petty that way.

"Hey. How've you been?" I asked.

"Well, if it isn't my little sis. How's New York?"

Geez. Was he as out of the loop as I was?

"I take it you haven't talked to Mom and Dad?" I asked.

I heard him peeing in the background. Gross. He always did that when he was on the phone with me.

"Haven't talked to them in a while, back when they sold the ranch," he said.

What the fuck.

"Yeah, well, I left New York to come to the ranch around the same time they were on the road, working their way to New York to pay a visit to me. So, I was pretty surprised when I arrived to find that Flood Creek Ranch was no longer owned by the Whitaker family."

He guffawed. "No shit. That's how you found out? I know Mom and Dad had said not to tell you so they could surprise you. Oops. They've been on the road for awhile, doing their RV thing."

Glad he thought it was funny.

"So where are you now? Back in New York? Did you see Mom and Dad?"

I pulled into the parking space behind the florist. I

needed to wrap up my call. "No, Buddy, I'm still in Flood Creek."

"What? Where the hell are you staying? Melanie's?"

And I'd thought I was out of the loop.

"No, I'm staying at the ranch. Roman let me have my own room back, at least for the time being."

Buddy sucked in his breath. "Are you fucking kidding me?" he snapped.

"Yeah. Guess he felt sorry for me." I laughed weakly.

"What the fuck, Ruby Lee? You get all the breaks."

What? Me? Breaks?

"Mom and Dad sell, and you still get to stay there. Roman and the guys never would have helped me out that way."

"Of course they would," I snapped back. "I mean, Cam is staying in your old bedroom. They'd welcome you back for sure."

"No, they would not. For one, I had a falling out with Cam long ago. He doesn't have anything to do with me."

That must have been why Cam said they'd been out of touch.

"Oh. Sorry to hear that, Buddy."

He huffed impatiently, cutting me off before I could ask any more questions. "Rubes, I gotta go. Say hi to everyone. Well, everyone who still likes me."

He laughed and hung up.

I MADE my deliveries in a somewhat robotic state, my brother's news having dampened some of the excitement of my morning sex with Jameson, and the little thrill I'd gotten from delivering flowers from a nameless paramour to Roman's ex-wife. She hadn't seen me, fortunately, because I wasn't sure how I'd answer all her questions while thinking about what a fool she was for letting a nice guy like Roman go. Turned out she and her kids were staying at her father's ranch and it was he, an elderly patrician man, who'd answered the door. He had no idea who I was, nor was he interested.

But he did tip me five bucks.

I vowed not to tell Roman about the flowers. It wasn't my place, and as Erin had stressed on many an occasion, we were discreet about who was sending what to whom. If anyone thought she was the source of any town gossip, her business would dry up fast.

Guess there was a lot of hanky panky going on in Flood Creek.

And when I thought about it, I was part of that.

When I'd finished for the day and confirmed with Erin that there was nothing more she needed help with, I headed over to the Flood Creek School to call on Mrs. Everett, Jameson's mother. He'd hinted around I should go say hi to her, and this was the first chance I'd gotten.

She was a lovely woman, bravely having done a bang-up job as single mom after Jameson's dad had bailed. She was now principal of the only school in town, the one I'd attended all the way from grade one through twelve.

Yup, it was that small of a school.

When the old, absent-minded school secretary ushered me into her office, Mrs. Everett jumped up from her chair and embraced me like I was her long-lost daughter.

"Oh, sweetie," she gushed, holding me at arms' length, "what a beautiful woman you've turned out to be."

She gestured toward one of the chairs facing her desk, a chair where countless numbers of parents had sat over the years to hear good news and bad news about their kids. "Take a seat. Let's catch up."

"You look great too, Mrs. Everett. You haven't changed a bit."

She waved a hand at my compliment and mumbled something about menopause not being kind. Then her face brightened.

"Thank you, sweetie. Say, Jameson tells me you're staying at the ranch. I'm so glad. And I bet they're all thrilled to have you."

Jameson better fucking be thrilled after this morning.

"Yes, ma'am, I think they are. It's very generous of them to let me stay for a bit."

Her eyes brightened and it occurred to me she knew my stay with the guys hadn't been completely platonic, at least not with her son. "Seems like the old spark might still be there, huh?" she suggested with a shimmy of her shoulders.

Oh shit. She was going there.

"I don't know about that, Mrs. Everett,—"

She laughed. "Just kidding," she interrupted.

As if on cue, the secretary wobbled in toward me and

stopped. "Joanie, the cafeteria delivery truck is here," she said, looking directly at me.

"Mrs. Phelps, that's Ruby Lee. Ruby Lee Whitaker. *I'm* Joanie, honey."

Mrs. Phelps looked between the two of us, confused, turned around without a word, and left.

Mrs. Everett laughed again. "Oh, Mrs. Phelps is getting on in years. But she's still an invaluable part of our team."

Mrs. Phelps had been old when I was in high school. Jesus.

Mrs. Everett stood, walking around the front of her desk and propping her butt on a corner. "Ruby Lee, I'd love to have you by to talk to some of the kids in the upper school about your experiences in New York. In fact, maybe we can have you come to one or two of our classes and discuss the business world that you worked in. Would you be interested in that?"

A thousand reasons to say no raced through my mind, not the least of which was that I hadn't exactly set the New York business world on fire with my talent or acumen. I wasn't sure what I'd share that didn't have to do with the best ways to manage a psychotic, abusive boss.

I stood up to go, good. "Sure. Happy to. Sounds like fun."

She threw her arms around me again, and dashed out to meet the cafeteria delivery truck, leaving Mrs. Phelps looking between the two of us, unsure of what the hell was going on.

23

CAM

"Yo, Jameson."

I knocked on the door to his bunkhouse suite, and let myself in. We didn't lock doors much at the ranch, although I imagined that when the day came when we were finally permitted to allow guests, that would change.

Not that I was inherently distrustful of anyone, much less people who wanted a ranch vacation, but by opening up the place to the public, it was impossible that everyone who joined us would be an honest, upstanding citizen. Plain and simple, there were assholes out there, which was why the lock and key were invented.

Jameson came out of the bathroom with a towel

wrapped around his waist, rubbing his hair dry with another.

"Hey, Cam. Want a beer?" He headed over to the fridge.

With Roman minutes away from arriving, it was surprising Jameson wasn't ready yet for our meeting. But he'd been a little late for most everything all day, and as he handed me a beer, he tried to hide a yawn.

Somebody had a late night.

"Better get dressed, dude, you know Roman likes to start on time."

We might all three be business partners, but with Roman holding the largest share of the ranch, and the fact that he was the oldest, Jameson and I deferred to him a great deal. Hell, the man had seen us grow up, so we were still getting used to seeing him as a peer.

At my prodding, Jameson moved a little faster. I watched him hustle over to his bed and tidy it up to make it somewhat presentable, when I spotted something on the nightstand that was definitely not his.

It was a woman's sweater that looked a lot like the one Ruby had been wearing the day before when she'd had her blow up in the kitchen.

Well, well.

I had no claim on Ruby, but I couldn't say I didn't feel a twinge of something when I realized the reason Jameson was so out of sorts was that he'd had her over and probably spent the night with her too.

I knew all three of us were attracted to her, and that and least two of us always had been—Jameson and me.

Sure, I'd had my high school girlfriend, but I'd always pined for Ruby, who was swept away before anyone else had a chance.

And she might have been Roman's babysitter, but he did confess that once he caught her watching him get dressed. He'd almost said something to her but knew that all it would do was serve to humiliate her and besides, she was underage. He wasn't touching that shit with a ten-foot pole.

Since Ruby had been back in town, she'd been with each of us. In any other group, that would have been a no-no. But I wanted to believe we guys were cool. If and when jealousy reared its head, we'd cop to it and address it.

What would come out of the three of us being interested in her? I had no idea. I suspected she was a traditional sort of girl, probably just sowing some wild oats before she left town for a place more her speed than Flood Creek.

But we guys still needed to talk. We didn't let things get in the way of our partnership, having vowed to be open and honest from the beginning.

"Looks like someone had an overnight guest," I said just as Roman arrived.

Jameson went to get another beer.

"I sure did." He pulled the tab and it opened with a loud *crack*. He passed it to Roman.

We took our usual seats on the heavy leather chairs gathered around Jameson's fireplace, and he lit a match to get the fire going.

"No shit. You had a guest, huh?" Roman grinned from ear to ear.

Jameson nodded. "I did. And it was our lovely Ruby, for anyone who's wondering."

Guess they'd made up with each other and then some after that big blowout.

Roman slapped his thigh. "Well, aren't you the lucky bastard?"

Jameson stretched his arms overhead. "I feel pretty fucking lucky, if you must know the truth."

Roman looked my way. "Cam. You're being awfully quiet."

Jameson leaned forward in his chair before I could say anything. "Guys. I have no claim on Ruby. I've seen the way she looks at each of us, and I have no doubt there's something there. I propose we have a little chat with her. See if she might be interested in an unconventional sort of arrangement."

Well, damn. I'd never really considered anything like that. But I was glad we were all honest with each other. It was the only way to operate.

Roman and Jameson moved on to the discussion of our permits, or rather, the lack of them.

"This is what I propose we do," Roman said. "Let's take a look at the six-member board. Each of us will take two members and have small, one-on-one meetings with the ones we have the best relationships with. We'll go over the business plan, the results of the environmental impact report we commissioned, and get solid feedback on any objections anybody has."

"I like it," I said. "We need to know what their beef is with our plans if we want to make any progress."

Roman shook his head. "It's total bullshit that they've put us off as long as they have, but if this doesn't break the stalemate, it'll be time to set our attorneys loose on them."

It sounded like a good plan to me, and one that had better fucking work. I hadn't invested my last dime in this place to keep it just as it was.

None of us had.

24

CAM

"Mrs. Phelps, do you know where I can find Ruby Whitaker?"

The old school secretary looked me up and down with a scowl, even though I'd taken off my cowboy hat. When I was growing up, she'd been infamous for being grouchy. Not much had changed.

"No, I do not," she barked, and went back to her typewriter.

Typewriter. Not computer.

"Mrs. Phelps, do you mind if I say hello to Mrs. Everett?" I asked, pointing toward the principal's office.

She waved without looking up. "Suit yourself, young man."

I poked my head into the principal's office, which I

probably hadn't been in since I was last a student there. And in trouble for some bone-headed infraction.

"Hi, Mrs. Everett."

She looked up from her computer.

"Cam. How nice to see you," she said, smiling. "Come in."

I entered the office slowly, as if I might be getting into trouble again after so many years. "It's so funny to see you in here, after all those years as my math teacher."

"I know what you mean. Some mornings I walk in and go to my old classroom before I remember where I'm supposed to be. Say, how's everything at the ranch? How's Jameson? I haven't seen him in a couple weeks."

I exhaled a long breath. "We're still dealing with permitting issues. I don't know what the planning board has against us, but it's a biggie."

She clicked her tongue. "Jerks. They're a bunch of power-hungry jerks. Let me know if there's anything I can do. So, what brings you by today?"

"I was going to stop in and see Ruby. I understand she was talking to a group of kids."

She pointed toward the back of the building as if I hadn't spent twelve years of my life in the place. "Room eleven. End of the hall."

"Thanks, Mrs. Everett. See you soon."

She waved at me and went back to her computer. I walked past Mrs. Phelps, who didn't even look up.

I headed down the hall, realizing the place smelled exactly as it did the day I graduated. The linoleum floor tile was the same, if a little more warped, and the bulletin boards outside each classroom were still littered with years of layers of construction paper.

"Cam! Hi. What are you doing here?"

Missy Folger jumped out of a classroom door as if she'd been waiting for me.

"Hey, Missy, are you teaching here now?" I asked.

She bounced in her platform shoes, her blonde hair swinging around her face. "Yeah. I took a job as the first grade teacher last year after Caldwell *finally* retired."

She rolled her eyes.

I looked into the classroom she'd just popped out of and about twenty first graders were craning their necks to see where their teacher had disappeared to.

I gestured toward her class with my thumb. "Missy, don't you have to get back—"

She giggled. "Course I do. But it's just so nice to see you. I mean, I haven't seen you out and about in ages and it would be so nice to hang out sometime—"

Just then, Ruby emerged from the seventh grade classroom, and spotted me.

Thank goodness.

"Cam!" she called, waving with a big smile.

The smile on Missy's face dissolved.

"Whatcha doing here?" Ruby asked.

Missy crossed her arms, looking between the two of us.

"Well, I was coming to see you talk to the seventh grade class, but I guess I'm too late."

Ruby waved her hand. "Oh lord. I don't know if I told

those kids a single thing they were interested in. I'm just glad it's over. And I'm glad you didn't see it."

She looked in Missy's direction and extended her hand. "I'm Ruby Whitaker."

Missy took her hand limply and smiled just as weakly. "I know who you are," she said, dropping Ruby's hand.

If she'd intended to insult Ruby, she missed by a long shot.

"Great. Shall we hit the road, Cam?" She turned to Missy. "We're going riding, so we need to take off. Nice meeting you," she chirped, and we headed toward the door.

"Sorry I missed your talk, Ruby. I really wanted to see it."

She laughed. "No, you did not. It was not only not memorable, but I'm pretty sure I turned those kids off to a career in business with my incoherent babbling."

I seriously doubted she'd embarrassed herself quite the way she was claiming. But hell, I hated public speaking too.

"So, how are you feeling about riding?" I asked.

I knew she hadn't been on a horse in years. It wasn't always easy to just get back on. You don't know what level you'll be, but you do know it won't be where you were when you last rode.

She took a deep breath. "I'm excited, but also a little nervous."

"Don't worry. We'll take it slow. Let's get back to the house so you can change."

25

CAM

I WAITED OUT FRONT WHILE RUBY GOT READY. I WAS afraid that if I went inside, I might follow her to her room, and who knows what might happen from there. But I was pretty sure we never would have made it to the stables that day.

It was only a few minutes before she came back outside, and I have to say, she was cute as hell in her blue jeans, plaid shirt, and cowboy boots.

"Hey, all you need is a hat." I ruffled up her hair.

She pointed. "It's funny. These boots were in my old closet, but the hat I got for my sixteenth birthday wasn't there."

"Well, I'm sure we can find one for you if you want."

When we pulled up to the stables fifteen minutes later, Ruby pointed. "There's that weird guy."

"Who, Roley? He's harmless. Just kind of shy and awkward. I had him get the horses ready for us."

We watched him walk around the back of the stables, glancing over his shoulder several times. He was definitely the nervous type, of that I was sure.

But Ruby had a serious frown on her face. "He's creepy, Cam. He stares, but he won't say hi, even when I call after him."

"You know how ranch hands are, Ruby, kind of an odd lot. But as long as they do the work we need them to, we keep them around. Well, that and as long as they don't make any trouble, either. If he continues to make you uncomfortable, let me or the guys know. We don't want that happening."

She gave me her lovely smile, and my dick twitched a little.

"Okay. So, I have you riding Sunshine today."

She walked over to the horse and began to pet her nose. "Aren't you just the prettiest thing?" she cooed.

Sunshine butted her head against Ruby, and it looked like they might be great friends.

After about ten minutes of our trail ride, I had Ruby pull up next to me. "How're you feeling?"

She beamed. "Incredible. So awesome."

Ruby was beautiful by any measure but seeing her up there on Sunshine was mind-blowing. As her confidence came back, I could see she was a good rider and was even more stunning in the saddle.

We continued in silence for another twenty minutes. "What do you say we take a break over there?" I asked, pointing to a gorgeous old oak casting a shadow perfect for hiding from the bright sun.

I helped Ruby dismount and we lay on our backs on the soft ground, looking up at the bits of sun breaking through the wavering leaves.

"Okay, now I have a question for *you*," I said.

She leaned up on one elbow. Fuck, I was dying to kiss her.

"Fair enough. What do you want to know?"

I was hoping I wouldn't piss her off. "What are you really doing back here in Flood Creek? This is longer than just a vacation."

She smiled. "You're right. I'll level with you. I got fired by an abusive psycho boss. And I'm fine with that. I couldn't take her shit anymore, and I'm not going back, either. That's why I came here. But now that my parents are gone, I'm not sure what I'll do. I can't stay at the ranch forever." She laughed sadly.

I rolled over on my side and ran a finger over her smooth cheek. "Actually, we guys would love it if you stayed."

She raised her head and opened her mouth to say something, but I kissed her before she could. Her head snapped back and she smiled, then pulled me closer.

Right there in the grass on a gorgeous Montana day, I hovered over Ruby Whitaker, enjoying her lovely lips, the ones I'd dreamed about since I was old enough to like girls. I gently pulled her shirt out of her jeans, and placed my hand on her warm stomach when a shadow passed over us.

We looked up to see Roman staring down at us, holding his horse's bridle.

"What the hell are you two doing?" he barked.

I bit my tongue to keep from laughing. I knew what he was up to.

Ruby sat up, tucking her shirt back in and straightening her hair. "Oh hi, Roman. We weren't doing anything."

He stood glaring at us, his lips pressed together tightly, until he couldn't hold it any longer and burst out laughing. "Oh my god, Ruby. I'm sorry. I was just messing with you."

He took a seat on the grass with us, and Ruby reached out to play-smack him.

"Jerk."

He was still laughing. "You should have seen your face. You looked like a little kid in trouble."

She rolled her eyes. "Whatever. I'll get even with you when you least expect it. Mark my words."

"Okay, darlin'. I've been warned. But hey, didn't mean to interrupt your fun time."

Ruby looked between the two of us, trying to figure out what was going on. Then, a wash of realization lit up her face.

She was no dummy.

"I just kissed Cam," she said. "Now, it's your turn."

He leaned toward her, put a hand behind her head, and kissed her hard.

Fuck yeah. I'd be lying if I didn't admit I loved watching. Well, not as much as I loved playing. But watching could be fucking hot.

Then, Ruby turned back to me, and I pulled her over for a kiss.

Had she ever been with two guys? I somehow doubted it.

While my kisses moved from her lips to her temples and down the sides of her neck, Roman opened her blouse and removed her bra. Next, he tackled her boots and jeans, and in a moment our lovely girl was butt naked in the beautiful outdoors, sexy as all hell.

She stopped for a moment and looked at us. "Oh my. I'm naked. And you guys are dressed. What are we going to do about that?"

I knew just what I needed to do. I knelt between her legs and buried my face in her pussy, which by now was soaked with her excitement.

"Oh my god, Cam," she breathed.

Roman resumed kissing her and playing with her tits while he opened his jeans and directed her hand to his cock. She stroked him slowly, speeding up when I entered her with two fingers and fucked her with them.

My own cock was fully erect, straining against my blue jeans. Unzipping my pants allowed me to relieve some of the pressure.

I continued lapping Ruby's pussy, zeroing in on her clit while I moved my fingers in and out. She writhed under me in the grass and kept working Roman's cock.

"Ruby, baby, I want to fuck you," I said.

She smiled at me and nodded.

Roman helped her to her knees, while I sheathed myself with a condom I'd grabbed from my wallet. While I got behind her, Roman kneeled in front, opening his pants all the way. With one of us behind her and one in front, she was about to be seriously tag teamed. She opened her mouth wide and took Roman deep.

To see her most private parts, I opened her pussy lips, and hell if she wasn't beautiful down there. I pressed against her opening, and she thrust back on me like a greedy little animal.

That turned me on so much I drove into her until my balls smacked against her wet slit.

"Mmmm," she groaned through her mouthful of Roman.

I gripped her hips and drove her hard, pushing her into Roman's dick.

His eyes were closed and with his hands on her head, he rocked his hips back and forth, fucking her face and pushing her back into me.

"Goddamn, baby," he groaned, and held his cock in her mouth until she couldn't swallow any more.

At the same time, my own orgasm was building, but I was waiting for Ruby. Turned out I didn't need to for very long.

"Fuck me, Cam, please fuck me," she rasped, groaning and bucking her head.

Just as her pussy squeezed me almost until it hurt, I pushed into her one last time and exploded with a groan, every inch of my being on fire.

We all collapsed under the oak tree, the horses grazing here and there, until a couple raindrops splattered on us through the canopy of overhead leaves.

"Uh oh," Ruby said, jumping up to dress.

We got back on our horses. But even in that short amount of time, the rain had turned into a steady drizzle.

If we didn't pick up the pace it would take a good half hour to get back to the barn, and it would be a miserable half hour for everyone except the horses.

"Are you comfortable riding a little faster?" I asked Ruby, now riding between Roman and myself.

She nodded, her wet hair sticking to her face. "I think so. Let's do it."

That's my girl. She might be nearly soaked to the skin, but she looked damn cute and was willing to test her riding skills.

We worked our way up to a trot, Roman in front and me behind. I smiled as I watched Ruby shift in her saddle, trying to get comfortable.

That will happen when you've been properly fucked.

26

RUBY

I was actually back on a horse.

If those New Yorkers could see me now.

I hadn't spoken to Posey in a while, who I was pretty sure was in Paris with our other girlfriends running around, eating, shopping, and doing all the things one did there. When she'd first told me about the trip, I felt a pang over having to miss it. The reality of my having bailed on New York, and all the things I was going to miss, had finally set in. Despite the work drama, New York had been fun while it lasted.

But I wouldn't trade Flood Creek for anything, now.

Roman, Cam, and I had our horses at a slow trot to get back to the stables before we started shivering with hypothermia. While the guys could have ridden a lot faster, they were happy to wait for me, rusty as my riding was. I told them they didn't need to, that I knew my way around the ranch at least as well as they did, but they stayed with me.

There was just something about cowboys that melted the heart. I mean, if one of them had an umbrella, he'd probably ride next to me and hold it over my head. I'd be hard-pressed to find that in New York. To think I'd believed guys there were the pot of gold at the end of the rainbow. Boy, had I been off the mark on that one.

And it was a good thing I couldn't go faster than a trot. Messing around with the guys under the oak tree had left me a little… sensitive. Roman had turned around at one point and caught me trying to find a comfortable position in the saddle and smiled wickedly.

Yeah, go ahead and laugh, buddy.

I was happy we were riding in single file. I didn't want them to see my face as I thought over what we'd just done. I'd never been with two guys at once, and I had to say, *mind blown.*

I'd had various girlfriends in New York who were in the ménage scene, and they talked about it like it was the best thing on the planet.

Now I knew why.

Having two sexy, strong, powerful cowboys work me over was the stuff girls dream of, and practically all I could think about was when we were going to do it again. I was like a greedy little animal. I just wanted more.

I had no idea what would come of messing around with the guys, but while it lasted, it was freaking beautiful. They'd awakened something in me, and I hoped they didn't end up regretting it.

Shit, I hoped I didn't end up regretting it.

So far, they were amazingly cool. Freakishly cool, actually. As if they'd done this sort of group activity before. I wanted to know more.

Or not. I could just enjoy myself.

When we got back to the stables, I spotted Roley meandering around, staring, then quickly looking away. Roman and Cam, occupied with getting the horses cleaned up, didn't notice.

I guess I just needed to chalk it up to his being a weird dude. But no woman liked being stared at. It was an aggressive move that any man with brains knew better than to pull. But two could play that game. I stared right back at him. If I ever got close enough to actually speak to him, I planned to tell him to take a chill pill.

As I started to clean Sunshine, it felt good to have some time to myself in her stall. I needed to figure out what the hell I was doing in Flood Creek.

As low-stress as delivering flowers for Erin was, it wasn't going to last. There was no way it could. I'd get bored. But I wasn't sure what else I might do. After all, I'd pretty much flopped in the business world.

In fact, my boss Sylvie had reminded me of that just yesterday.

I was shocked when I saw her number ringing on my

cell. I almost didn't answer but my curiosity—and pride —got the better of me.

"Hello?" I said, as if I didn't know who it was.

"Ruby," she boomed, like she always did, "how is Nebraska?"

I had to sit down for this one.

"Oh, hi Sylvie," I said, faking surprise. "I'm not in Nebraska."

In the background, her stiletto heels clicked across the floor as her office door closed. What the hell was she up to that she needed privacy?

"Right! I mean North Dakota."

Still wrong.

"I'm not in North Dakota either," I said flatly.

She sighed deeply, like it was my fault she didn't know one Western state from another. "Oh Ruby, where the fuck are you, then?" she snapped.

And this was why I left New York.

"Sylvie, is there anything I can do for you? I'm guessing you called for a reason other than to figure out which state I'm in."

Holy crap. I'd never been so sassy with her.

She was silent for a moment, probably blown away at my newfound assertiveness. I know I was.

"Ruby," she started, clearing her throat, "we need you back here at the office."

Damn. That was it? She wasn't even going to ask nicely?

No, of course not. Sylvie didn't ask nicely for

anything. She just demanded things. And somehow, she always got them.

If I pulled that, I'd get laughed at right in the face.

"Gosh, Sylvie, I'm not sure how useful I could be to the office, given that I'm in *Montana*, two thousand miles away."

She sucked in her breath. "I've tried two other assistants and they just didn't work out. I need you."

"Oh, I thought you said the *office* needed me. But it's actually *you* who does?"

I was pushing it, I knew. But what the hell did I have to lose? She was never going to see my ass again, and she was about to find that out.

"Ruby, I don't like that tone. I am offering your job back. I might even be able to swing a little raise for you. But don't act like you are some sort of savior. Think about it. Do you really think you could do any better than working for me?"

And there we had it. The insult I'd been waiting for.

Since I'd been a few weeks without her abuse, hearing it again pissed me off. I'd lived with that bullshit every day of my life working for her.

I didn't respond. I mean, what was there to say to a narcissistic, cunty bitch?

And I never called anyone that. But if it were defined in the dictionary, Sylvie's face would be right next to it—her puffed-up, Botoxed face.

"Gee, Sylvie, thanks for the offer. And thanks for the insult. You've done a great job of reminding me why I so happily left you and the agency. I hope you find someone else to abuse as your assistant. But I can promise you, no one will ever stay for very long with the way you treat people."

I swiped my phone closed, shaking, not so much for telling her off, but for burning a bridge so absolutely and completely. There would be no going back. *Ever.*

Which I guess was the idea.

The longer I stuck around Flood Creek, the more I marveled that I'd ever put up with that garbage.

"Hey, you almost done?" Cam asked, poking his head into Sunshine's stall.

I wiped a drop of sweat off my temple. It had been a long time since I'd put away a horse, and I was a little on the slow side.

"Almost done brushing. I just have to clean her hooves."

"Let's do that later. I want to let her graze for a bit."

I pushed the wet hair off my face. "I must look pathetic."

Cam took my face in his hands. "You look natural. And that's the most beautiful thing of all."

ON MY WAY TO pick up my flower deliveries, I stopped by the Flood Creek School.

"Hi, Mrs. Phelps. Can I go in to see Mrs. Everett?" I asked.

She looked up from her typewriter, where it looked

like she was trying to change the ribbon—where did you even get those anymore?—and glared at me.

"Very funny, Joanie."

Good lord. Did she still think I was Mrs. Everett? No matter, I decided to help myself to the principal's office.

I knocked softly on the doorjamb. "Mrs. Everett? Do you have a moment?"

Her face brightened and she waved me in. "Hi, Ruby."

"Hi there. Hey, Mrs. Phelps still thinks I am you."

She waved her hand. "Oh my gosh. I don't know what we're going to do with her. We just can't bear to let her go. What would she do with her days? So we keep her on and occasionally get a little work out of her. On the days she doesn't scare people off."

Gotta love small town life.

"So, I've come to talk to you about a couple things."

Her face grew serious and she pushed her glasses up on her head. "I'm all ears."

I'd always adored Jameson's mom. That's what she had been to me when we were teenagers. Not a schoolteacher, but a surrogate mom who was always looking out for me. I could trust her then, and I could trust her now.

"Mrs. Everett, I need to find a job. Something more than delivering flowers. I mean, I like working for Erin, but I can't do that long term."

She studied me for a moment. "I was wondering if you were here in Flood Creek just for a visit, or something longer term. What happened in New York?"

Of course she was going to want to know that story.

But how much should I tell her?

Oh, what the fuck.

"I got fired. But it was a godsend. I couldn't take it anymore. I had a crazy, abusive boss."

"Why didn't you look for another job?" she asked.

Fair question.

"I… just didn't think, when all was said and done, that any other job in New York would be much better. I had to get out of there."

She nodded.

"I just wanted to be home for a while. With my parents. At the ranch."

Those words, and my disappointment, caught up to me and my eyes filled with tears.

Shit.

But it was Mrs. Everett. She could be trusted.

"I can see that's been hard on you, getting here and finding out your parents had moved on."

I nodded, watching big fat tears dribble onto my folded hands.

"It's a loss for you. Even if you're staying at the ranch, it's not like it was," she said softly.

Ugh. Why did she have to be so nice? Now the water-works were really flowing.

All I could do was nod in agreement.

She passed me a tissue and I dabbed my eyes. "Sorry, Mrs. Everett. Didn't know I was going to lose it like this." I cleared my throat and rolled my shoulders to shake the emotion off.

"And about New York not working out the way you'd

hoped, there's no shame in that. In fact, it's amazing you even gave it a shot. You're from a small Western town. How many people like yourself did you meet in New York? I'd guess not many."

I laughed. "I never met a single one there. But everyone I did meet was very curious about ranch life. They always asked if they could come back with me."

Her eyebrows rose. "Maybe they can, if the plans for the ranch work out."

That would be glorious. All my New York friends on *my* turf, where I'd show them the ropes.

Literally.

"I may have something for you, Ruby, work-wise. It's temporary, but you may like it. The art teacher is going on maternity leave. You'd have to follow the lesson plans she designed, but it could be a fun gig."

Oh my god. Teaching art to kids. My spirits instantly lifted.

"That sounds incredible. I'm a little artsy. If her lessons are all planned out, I could probably handle implementing them."

"I think you're *a lot artsy*. I remember your mother's paintings, and how she was teaching you, even though you were more interested in chasing boys."

She was right. Mom thought I had the same talent for fine art that she did, but couldn't get me to sit still.

And now her paintings were in all the bunkhouse guest rooms.

"You could sit in on her classes for a bit to get a feel

for the work. If she feels you can handle it, we'll bring you on board."

I jumped to my feet. "Thank you, Mrs. Everett. Thank you so much. I'm thrilled."

I ran back out to my truck and raced back to the ranch. All I could think was how I wanted to share the good news with the guys.

My guys.

27

ROMAN

"It's so crazy that you bought my parents' boat."

"It came with the whole deal. I knew I wouldn't have much chance to use it, but I figured what the hell. Might as well take it."

I steered the old houseboat across the lake.

Ruby looked around, excited, which I loved to see. "I used to come here as a little kid. Nothing has changed. Not the snack bar, not the lifeguard chairs, nothing."

Even better, given that it was a weekday, we had the place to ourselves.

Which was no accident. We'd wanted some quiet time on the water with Ruby. We had important things to discuss.

And do.

We motored over to a little cove and before I even finished dropping the anchor, a bunch of hooting and hollering came from the back of the boat, followed by two big splashes. Both Cam and Jameson broke the surface moments later, smiling and splashing each other with the chilly May water.

Yeah, we really needed this day. All of us.

"So, you sound excited about your job at the school."

Ruby's eyes brightened. "Oh yeah. I mean, it's not permanent or anything, but I think it will be a lot of fun. Who wouldn't want to teach art, you know?"

She was so beautiful in the sun, her skin glowing. She reached to adjust the red bandana holding her hair back, and looked up at me with her killer smile.

We followed Cam and Jameson's swimming progress toward the middle of the lake, where they appeared to be racing.

"Do you ever miss being married, Roman?"

I hadn't been expecting *that.*

But I nodded. "Yes, I do. Even though it's best that my wife and I went our separate ways, when you're used to having a partner and family, and one day you wake up and all that is gone, it's a big adjustment. And not a fun one."

"Is that why you decided to buy Flood Creek? For something different?"

Perceptive. I was impressed.

"Yeah. I wanted a project. I'd done all I could with my little ranch, so merging the two seemed like the perfect thing to do. And Jameson had all these amazing ideas for expanding into tourism. As soon as we get our permits, we'll finish our build, which Cam will be heading up, and see what happens."

There were a couple loud thumps at the back of the boat as Cam and Jameson returned from their swim.

"Hey, can I get a towel?" Cam called.

Ruby jumped up, grabbing two towels off a chair, and tossed them to the guys.

"Eh, I don't need one," Jameson said, stripping off his bathing suit and wringing it out over the railing. He laid it out flat to dry and joined us in the cabin.

"You might want to put some pants on, dude," Cam said.

We all looked at Ruby.

She shrugged. "Doesn't make any difference to me."

"Jameson's become quite the nudist," Cam said. "We had to share a hotel room for a cattle auction, and he was just balls out the whole time."

Lovely.

Jameson huffed and rolled his eyes. "Okay, Cam. If it bothers you that much..." He took one of the towels and wrapped it around his waist.

Cam sat on the bench seat opposite Ruby and leaned forward on his elbows. "So Ruby, we have something to talk to you about."

She wrinkled her nose. "Me? Really?"

He nodded. "I touched on this the other day. You might have figured this out already, but we like you. We all like you. Quite a lot."

Her faced turned an adorable shade of pink. She opened her mouth to speak, but at first nothing came out. Then, she seemed to get her footing.

"I don't know what to say. Thank you, I guess." She giggled nervously.

Jameson jumped in. "We have a proposition for you. We'd all like to date you. Together."

She wrinkled her brow and looked from one of us to the other, as if she were asking for clarification. I didn't blame her.

"It's unconventional. We know that. But we think it can be great, obviously, if you're okay with it. In fact, you have to be more than okay with it. You have to want it," I added.

"I… I am not sure what to say. I guess I don't really understand."

It was to be expected.

"We'd like for you to stick around Flood Creek, and if you're open to it, be in a relationship with all three of us," Cam said.

A smile spread over her face. "So… you guys would essentially be my own personal harem?"

I'd heard it called that before.

We looked at each other and nodded.

"You don't have to decide right now. Think about it for a bit," Jameson said.

Then he got up and walked to Ruby, gently pulling her up by her shoulders. He put his hands on either side of her face and kissed her.

Not one to be left out, I positioned myself behind her,

my hands wandering under her T-shirt until I found her breasts. I drew them out of her bra and pulled on her nipples until she squirmed.

Cam came up on the other side and proceeded to open her jeans. He reached his hand inside and moved it between her legs.

Her eyes fluttered closed as the three of us worked her over.

"Hey, let's move to the bedroom," I suggested.

Jameson and Cam each took one of Ruby's hands, leading her to a bed in one of the sleeping rooms. As soon as we had her in there, I removed her sneakers and socks and lowered her jeans. While I did that, Cam lifted her T-shirt over her head and removed her bra with a flick of his wrist.

Then, he lay back on the bed, opening his pants and stroking his erection. "C'mere, Ruby," he said, gesturing with his chin. "Come sit on my face."

Fuck yeah.

She crawled over him and hovered her pussy just above his face. Cam gripped her thighs and pulled her down, licking her furiously from top to bottom.

"Oh god," she moaned, writhing on his face.

Jameson and I looked at each other and smiled.

Watching from behind, we had a perfect view of her wide open pussy and ass, neatly shaven and a lovely shade of pink. Jameson popped a finger in his mouth to get it wet, then moved behind Ruby and spread her ass cheeks wide. He ran his wet finger back and forth over her asshole, playing with it until he could penetrate her the smallest amount.

While he was doing this, I got on the bed in front of Ruby, where she was perfectly positioned to suck cock. I pulled my hard-on out of my jeans and held it for her. With Cam licking her pussy and Jameson working her ass, she opened wide for me, sucking me with a vigor I don't think I'd ever experienced. In minutes, my cum rushed from my balls to my dick, and I spurted hot and deep into her pretty mouth.

Cam moved from under her, where she remained on all fours. He waved me out of the way and took my place filling her mouth with his cock. She sucked eagerly, moaning with her mouth full.

Jameson continued working on her ass, and was now inside her up to his knuckle. She pressed back against him and he smiled. I'd never known an ass man like him. Who would have thought this combination cowboy-hippie would have such an anal fixation.

To help him along, I reached under Ruby and made circles on her hard clit. In response, she wiggled her hips and pressed into my hand.

"Fuck," Cam roared, pulling out of her mouth and coming against her cheek.

And before he was even finished, she started to shudder and scream. I quickly slipped a finger in her pussy to feel her come. With Jameson in her ass, both her holes were now filled. She reared against us while an orgasm bowled her over.

Jameson pulled out and walked to the nightstand,

returning with a condom and lube. He sheathed himself, then drenched his cock and Ruby's ass with the slippery liquid, and pressed himself against her tiny pink opening.

"Ughhhh," she groaned as he popped his cockhead inside her.

Her breath was hard and raspy and her head hung down, her mouth open.

"You okay, baby?" Jameson asked.

She pushed back a little further on him and nodded. "Yeah. I think so."

He gradually entered her ass, stopping frequently to let her adjust to his girth. I was amazed that, when he was fully seated inside her, she was able to take his whole dick.

I crawled across the bed, and put my face next to hers.

"You like it baby? You like a dick in your ass?" I whispered hotly in her ear.

"Mmmm. I do. I like it," she said, between gasps.

"Is it your first time?" I asked.

She nodded. "Yeah. And I like it. I want him to fuck my ass."

I looked up at Jameson. "Did you hear what the lady said?"

He pursed his lips and with a tight grip on her hips, began to pummel Ruby's behind. I took the opportunity to rub her clit to see if the two of us could bring her to orgasm again.

I didn't have to wait long.

Her head thrashed wildly and she pushed into both Jameson's cock and my hand. With a scream, she came, once again shuddering and convulsing until Jameson pulled out and she collapsed on the bed right into Cam's arms.

Fucking hot.

I didn't know whether she'd accept our proposal, but I bet she'd never forget that afternoon on the houseboat.

28

ROMAN

"HEY, ROLEY. HOW ARE THINGS?"

The ranch hand looked down at his shoes, shuffling uncomfortably just like he always did. He was a bit odd, but most itincrant guys like him marched to the beat of their own drum, anyway. I'd been dealing with men like this for years.

He kicked the ground with the tip of his cowboy boot, stirring up a little cloud of dust.

I needed to get on a call, but I reminded myself to be patient.

"What's on your mind, Roley?"

He finally looked up, meeting my gaze with a tilted head. The lines between his brows were pronounced, like he was carrying the weight of the world on his shoulders.

"Mr. Maxwell, it has come to my attention that I need to share something with you."

I gestured toward the house. "All right. Do you want to come and talk in my office, then?"

He shook his head hard. "No. No, I'd rather talk out here where we have privacy."

And that's when I began to feel a little uncomfortable. Actually, maybe a better word was uneasy. I didn't know why or how, but at that moment, something felt *off*.

It was the only way to put it.

"Mr. Maxwell, I gotta tell you, I know what you're up to."

That, I was not expecting.

So I waited. Give a man enough rope, and all that.

He looked up at me, apparently expecting me to react in a certain way. But I didn't. At all.

And how could I? I honestly had no idea what the hell he was talking about, aside from his accusatory tone.

Not the best way to kick off a conversation with me.

"Speak your mind, man," I said, trying to still the impatience in my voice. "Look, Roley, I got stuff to do—"

He looked off into the horizon and took a deep breath. "I know what you're doing with Ruby Lee. And I don't like it."

Well, I'd be damned.

"It's not right, sir. That perverted kind of thing has no place at Flood Creek Ranch, or anywhere, for that matter."

Perverted. It didn't take much imagination to guess he

was talking about sex, and more specifically the sex Cam, Jameson, and I had with her.

How the fuck did he find out?

And why did he give a damn, anyway.

Just as I was about to tell him to hit the road, and that his short-lived employment with Flood Creek Ranch was over, he continued. Digging himself in further, I might add.

I took a deep breath. "I appreciate your sharing your feelings with me Roley, but—"

"If you want to keep this quiet, sir, you're going to have to make it worth my while."

I almost laughed. Almost.

"Is that so? And if I don't make it worth your while?"

He shuffled again, clearly not used to extortion. But he sure as hell recognized an opportunity when he saw one.

"I'll be sure to let the whole town know about the perversions going on over here at the ranch."

And there it was. Fucking opportunist thinking he could make a fortune off the people who gave him a goddamn job.

On the tip of my tongue were the words *go to hell,* and *get the fuck out.* But my sensible side took over before my angry one did.

Thank goodness.

Not only did a creep like this need to be handled carefully, but he also needed to be taught a lesson.

Seriously. Did he really think he could fuck with us?

I took a deep breath, and made sure my expression

depicted grim unease. "Okay, Roley. I see what you are getting at. What do you want in return for your silence?"

I felt like I was in an episode of Magnum P.I.

"Well, sir, how much is my silence worth to you?"

He'd definitely been watching Magnum P.I.

I looked up at the blue sky, pretending to think. I needed to buy a little time. But I had some ideas. Some very good ideas.

"Can I think about it, Roley? You caught me off guard."

Which was all completely true.

"Yes, sir."

The respectful way he addressed me was in sharp contrast to his shakedown. He wasn't exactly a criminal mastermind.

He turned to walk away.

"Hey, Roley," I called.

"Yes, sir?"

"The pool needs cleaning. Can you take care of that for us?"

He turned up his nose. "Really? There ain't no pool cleaner?"

His nerve was epic.

"You are the pool cleaner, Roley. Ranch hands take care of the pool."

His eyes grew darker, and he was about to sass me when I cut him off.

"Roley, don't you want to see Ruby laying around in her bikini? I can assure you, she's quite a nice woman to look at."

Realization washed over his face, and he brightened. "Um. Okay. I'll get right on it."

And he took off.

Fucking asshole. He thought he had the upper hand?

I don't think so.

I stormed back to my office, beyond pissed that on top of everything else I had going on, I had to deal with a junior-level criminal. And I think what further angered me was not so much that he thought he could get one over on me and the guys, but that he'd hurt Ruby, who'd never done a damn thing to him.

I fell into my desk chair, getting more worked up by the moment. I picked up a heavy paperweight that Whit Whitaker had left behind, the rattle of a snake he'd been bitten by, now encased in a heavy block of yellowed acrylic like something made by a kid in arts and crafts.

I knew all this because he'd proudly told me.

I took the paperweight, because I was in the mood to do something violent, and chucked it hard against the far wall.

The ugly fucker still didn't break. But it did leave a big dent in the wall.

Out the back window I could see Roley sweeping the pool, providing me the opportunity to take care of business. I hopped in my truck and headed over to the bunkhouses. Not the nice ones, where Jameson now lived, but the rustic ones where guys like Roley camped out.

I had a plan.

29

RUBY

"Today's the big day, huh?"

It seriously was. In fact, it was such a big day that I'd felt on the edge of barfing since I'd woken up that morning.

And, as if she could read my mind, Mary rubbed my shoulder and gave me some tea. She bent down next to my ear. "I know you're excited honey, but try to eat a couple bites. It will help calm your nerves."

I wanted to jump up and hug her. She was looking after me just like she had when I was a kid. How did I get this lucky?

There I was, in my parents'—well, not parents' anymore—ranch house, sharing a breakfast table with three of the hottest cowboys who'd ever walked the face of the earth. And I could say that because I'd seen a cowboy or two.

With Mary feeding me, on top of everything else, my struggles in New York seemed pretty fucking far away.

"I am excited," I admitted. "Nervous, too."

Cam waved his hand. "What is there to be nervous about? It's just the Flood Creek School. Shit, you'll know everyone's kids there. We probably grew up with all their parents."

"Exactly. That's probably what she's nervous about," Jameson said. "She has to deal with all the assholes we grew up with."

God forbid. But on the other hand, if anyone gave me crap, I could always unleash Melanie on them. That girl had my back and then some. When she realized I would be teaching one of her kids, she immediately volunteered to help. All I could say to that, besides yes, was that I predicted she'd be at least as badly behaved as the kids in the class.

Speaking of which, I arrived at the school just as Melanie, with her littlest strapped to her chest, was coming out of the building after dropping off her three oldest.

"Hey, girl," she called.

She should probably have called me Miss Whitaker, at least around the school, but if I corrected her then I knew she never would.

"Hey, Mel. Isn't it early to drop the kids?"

She shrugged and patted the bald head of the one strapped to her chest. "If you had as many as I do, you'd be eager to get rid of them, too." She dropped her head back and cackled.

Oh my god.

Then, she play-slapped me. "I'm kidding! Jesus, you should have seen your face. They're at their music lessons."

That was just like Melanie.

"Look. Good luck on your first day. You need anything, you call me. I can be here in ten minutes. Now I gotta get home and feed this one before he tears my tit off. Christ, he eats like a linebacker."

I gave her quick hug without squashing the baby. "I'll see ya later. Probably after school."

She started walking away, but turned back and looked me up and down and pointed. "That blue is great on you. So much better than all that black shit you were wearing all the time. Cripes, I was waiting for you to show up with that awful Elvira black nail polish." She laughed again, and skipped down the school steps with the baby bouncing against her chest.

Damn. I used to wear black nail polish all the time.

I looked up at my old school, once a permanent fixture in my life, as important as the home I'd grown up in. And yet, when I left town, I'd barely given it another thought. I guess that's what you did when you wanted a new life. You closed out the things that had brought you comfort in the past so you didn't miss them too much. And now that I was face to face with the Flood Creek School, and was going to actually attempt to teach some of the kids there, that old feeling of comfort returned, washing over me like Mary's care at the breakfast table.

It was all so unexpected.

I stopped by the school office first. "Good morning, Mrs. Phelps."

This time, she was standing behind the counter, like a clerk waiting for customers.

"Hello," she said.

"Mrs. Phelps, I'm here to teach the art class. For Mrs. Boyer."

I'd worked with Sandy Boyer for several days before she'd given me the thumbs up. But honestly, I think that even if she'd given me the thumbs down, Mrs. Everett still would have hired me. It's not like Flood Creek was full of art teachers.

"Okay," Mrs. Phelps said, just looking at me.

I peered around the corner into Mrs. Everett's office, which was empty. "All right then, I'll just go down to the art room and get my things together."

"Okay," she said again.

Good grief.

I arrived in the second grade class a couple minutes early and watched their regular teacher with a reading lesson. They were all so cute and well-behaved, sitting up straight, raising their hands when they had questions, and waiting their turn to speak.

For some reason though, all that went out the window as soon as their teacher left me alone with them.

It started with a barrage of questions.

"Where's Mrs. Boyer? Did she have her baby?"

"She was so fat, she must be having two babies."

Laughter skittered through the room.

"Are you married? How old are you?"

"Are you having a baby?"

"Are you going to teach us anything fun? Mrs. Boyer always taught us fun stuff."

Boy, was I in over my head. I'd shadowed their regular teacher to learn how she implemented her lesson plans.

No one had taught me a thing about discipline. I'd assumed the kids would be good, like I'd been at that age.

Actually, I wasn't that good at that age. It was when I'd met Melanie, and developed a big mouth. And a smart mouth.

Memories of my second grade teacher came flooding back. I hadn't been an easy chatterbox to shut up, so I'd spent a lot of time sitting at a lone desk in the corner reserved for kids in need of a little isolation.

In this classroom, there was no such station. So, I created one.

I took an empty desk and chair and dragged them to the corner of the room. "Okay people, this desk is for those of you who don't know how to be quiet. It looks kind of lonely over there, so I hope none of you have to go sit at it. All by yourself. Alone. With no one near you."

The chatter in the room ceased.

Bingo. I had built the first weapon in my arsenal. I was on my way.

30

RUBY

When the teaching day was over, I ran to Mrs. Everett's office.

"Ruby, honey. How'd it go?" she asked, looking up from some paperwork.

I was ready to explode. "I loved it. So much fun!"

She breathed a sigh of relief and smiled. "Oh, thank god. I thought you'd like it, but not everyone takes a shine to teaching."

I didn't know if I did as much teaching as I did babysitting, but I still had a good time and the kids I'd taught weren't much trouble once they'd realized I was the alpha in the room.

To celebrate, I walked down the street to the Flood Creek Saloon to treat myself to a beer.

Had I been in New York, I would have splurged on a glass of champagne. But that was not the sort of thing one ordered in Flood Creek.

I texted the guys where I was, bursting to tell them about my day. Jameson replied right away saying he could be there in thirty minutes.

The saloon was fairly empty at that early hour, so I decided to call my parents and find out where they were and fill them in on all the new happenings. Just as I was about to hit *send*, there was a tap at my shoulder.

I turned to see none other than Dale something-or-other, the popular jock from my high school graduating class, standing there.

"Ruby Lee, I'd heard you were back in town."

Why would he care if I were around? He'd pretty much ignored me all through high school. Melanie and I had not been part of the popular crowd. I mean, we had our posse of friends, but we didn't have the social currency needed to be top-rung popular.

Which was fine with us.

"Hi, Dale. How've you been?"

He helped himself to the seat next to me and waved the bartender over. While I easily knew who he was, he'd lost his hair and gained a lot of weight.

"I'm good. And even better, now that I'm looking at you."

Ew.

I gave my best fake laugh. "Thanks, Dale. So are you still married to Trudy?"

He waved his hand like he'd just smelled something bad. "Oh, hell no. I dumped her ages ago."

He did not just say that.

Dick.

"Yeah. She got the kids, the house, the car. She got it all. Women always do," he said, holding his beer bottle so tightly I thought it might break.

I checked my watch. Jameson would be here in ten minutes. Hopefully, less.

Dale turned on his barstool to fully face me. I remained facing the bar.

"Can I just say, Ruby Lee, how great you look? I mean you were so chubby and, you know, basically unattractive growing up and look at you now."

Oh. My. God.

I had never imagined people like him actually existed.

"Where were you? New York was it? Did you get breast implants there? I hear they have the best plastic surgeons in the country—"

"Dale, I do not have breast implants, and further, I go by Ruby now—"

He slung an arm around my shoulder. "Look, Ruby Lee, don't be so darn sensitive. Hey, there's a movie I've been wanting to see. Why don't you come with me? It starts in an hour."

I wriggled my shoulders to get rid of him, but no luck. I tried to pick his hand up off my shoulder, but he just clung tighter and in fact placed a hand on my thigh and squeezed.

"Dale, I'd really appreciate if you—"

"Dale, I think she wants you to take your hands off her." Jameson's voice boomed behind me.

Ohthankgod.

Surprised, Dale lessened his grip, and I squirmed out from under him. But he wasn't completely discouraged. He looked Jameson up and down with a smirk.

Not a good move.

"Everett, why don't you get the hell out of here. Ruby Lee and I were having a conversation."

Jameson looked at me, and I shook my head slightly.

"Naw, Dale. I think it's time for you to go."

Dale jumped to his feet. "Fuck off, Jameson. You'd be nothing if you hadn't inherited your money. You didn't earn a bit of it."

Jameson looked down at his boots, hands on hips, and slowly shook his head.

The contrast between the two guys could not have been sharper. Dale was puffy and pale, whereas Jameson was tanned and buff. He looked infinitely healthier.

And hotter.

"Dale, I asked you nicely. Now, we aren't talking about me and my money. We're talking about your bothering Ruby. And since it doesn't seem like you're hearing me, I'll help you."

Holy shit. I slipped off my bar stool to move out of the way. I'd seen enough fights in my life to know when one was coming.

Dale twisted his face into pure ugliness. "You're such a loser, Everett, defending the former fat girl here. I mean, really," he said, addressing me, "do you think you can afford to be so picky?"

Jameson's eyes got dark, and I moved even further away. The bartender watched from his end of the bar, polishing glasses, looking excited to have some entertainment.

Before anyone realized what was going on, Jameson had grabbed Dale by the front of his shirt and jacket, yanking him toward the door.

"Get. The. Fuck. Out," he bellowed, pushing the door open with his elbow and depositing Dale on the sidewalk.

My heart pounded so hard I held on to the bar for balance. I was also turned on as hell.

Jameson shook his arms to dump some of his tension, and grabbed the barstool where Dale had been.

He leaned toward me, planting a kiss on my cheek. "Hey darlin'. How was teaching?"

WHAT A DAY. Jameson and I stuck around the saloon for a while longer, and I regaled him with my stories of outwitting a bunch of eight and nine-year-olds.

Who cared if they were mini-humans? They were fucking scary as hell.

We raced home, having received a text from Mary that she'd made her famous ribs and coleslaw, and when we pulled up in front of the house, creepy Roley was skulking around.

"Oh my god, there's that weird guy. Jameson, introduce us so he has to talk to me."

Jameson shrugged. "Okay. Sure." He waved at Roley. "Hey. Can you come here a sec?" he called.

Roley looked nervous and walked toward us slowly, mostly looking around as if he wanted an escape route.

"Roley," Jameson said, putting a hand on the man's shoulder, "I want you to meet Ruby Whitaker. Her family used to own the ranch."

He looked everywhere but at me.

Seriously strange.

Roman poked his head out the front door. I figured he'd seen us pull up. "Jameson, glad you're back."

The look on Roman's face pretty much said *we need to talk*, and Jameson headed over his way, leaving me with Roley.

Perfect.

"Roley, I noticed you avoiding me. I'm wondering why."

He looked into the distance, back at his boots, then up at me with pained eyes.

"Sorry, miss. But I don't talk to no whores."

31

JAMESON

"Close the door, will ya?"

Roman nodded at me to take a seat.

First thing I noticed was a big dent in the wall next to the picture window. Given that the walls were heavy wood and not drywall, something must have hit damn hard.

"Throwing shit again?"

I'd seen him pissed before. It wasn't pretty. Probably how he'd burned bridges with the Flood Creek planning board. Those chickens were now coming home to roost, so to speak, that was for damn sure. Those old bastards were fucking with our plans, and having a great time doing it.

Roman stood, towering over his desk. If he wasn't my business partner and friend, I might be intimidated.

Another thing that worked against him from time to time.

He took a deep breath. "We have an issue."

Well, shit. Just when I'd started to get my hopes up that we were making some progress with the planning board.

I shook my head. "Damn, Roman. There must be something we can do. We can't let those assholes drive Flood Creek back into the last century. It's bad enough they are blocking the rebuilding of the old hotel. That vacant, burned out lot is a disgraceful eyesore. I saw some kids playing in it the other day. Someone's going to get hurt."

Fuckers.

"Actually, it's not the planning board I'm talking about. Not today, anyway."

Huh?

"Seems our ranch hand Roley has become a bit of a problem."

"Roley?"

I looked out the window to where I'd left him talking with Ruby. The front door opened and slammed shut. She flew in, heading upstairs without a word. In the opposite direction, his skinny outline got smaller and smaller as he headed down the ranch road, probably back to his bunkhouse.

Had something happened? Had he done something to Ruby?

My heart slammed against my chest as adrenaline surged. "What is it, Roman? Does it have something to do with Ruby? Because she told me he was acting strange toward her. I swear, if he lays a finger on her, I'll kill him—"

With his arms crossed, Roman began to pace. "It does have to do with Ruby. Actually, it has to do with all of us."

Shit.

"He came to me earlier and let me know he was aware of our... relationship with Ruby. Said that if we didn't make it worth his while, he'd make everyone in town aware of our 'perverted' ways."

He used air quotes around 'perverted.'

Fucker.

He might not have touched Ruby, but I was still going to kill him. I rose to head out, but Roman stopped me.

"Hold up, hot head. I've got an idea that will be far more effective than beating the tar out of the punk. Not to mention, firing his ass and telling him to hit the road. That satisfaction will come later."

Not sure I was that patient. I'd already roughed up one asshole today. I wouldn't mind making it an even two.

And where did that loser get off having any kind of comment about our relationship with Ruby, much less passing judgment? That's what irked me the most. Ruby had never done a thing to him, and he was benefitting from the bounty of what her parents had taken years to build.

The fucking nerve.

I took my seat again before I threw something, like Roman had done earlier.

"Your reaction is about what mine was. I wanted to deck him and then throw him the hell out."

"The little pissant." I put my head in my hands and tried to take deep breaths. "What's your idea?"

Roman returned to his seat, too, and drummed his fingers on the desk. "We'll fire him, for sure. But first, we'll make sure he can't talk."

I burst out laughing. "How do we do that? Cut his tongue out?"

Roman smiled. "Not a bad idea. But here's what I'm thinking. Remember when Cam told us he thought Roley was stealing stuff from his father's junkyard on the other side of the state? He takes it all over and sells the scrap metal."

I vaguely remembered. Ranch hands came in all shapes and sizes, and pretty much nothing they did would faze me.

Some like Roley were thieving assholes. Others read fucking Shakespeare.

"Yeah. What about it?" I asked.

"We tell Roley his dad's coming to town to discuss doing some work with us and to see the property. He'll shit himself, thinking his dad will see his stash of stolen goods. We'll give him the chance to vacate the premises with his stuff if he promises to keep his mouth shut and leave the county."

Why hadn't I thought of that? It was perfect. We had

just enough dirt on the asshole to get rid of him with no harm done to anyone.

"I like it. We just need to fill in Cam, who I'm sure will be on board. He always thought Roley didn't pull his weight anyway."

Roman laughed. "No shit. I asked him to clean the leaves out of the pool and he was a whiny bitch about it."

"Good grief. That's the easiest job around here."

Roman shook his head. "Seriously. I needed to keep him busy while I snooped around the bunkhouse to see where he was keeping his stash. Turns out it's all in the old barn."

"You mean the one we don't use anymore?" I asked.

That fucker Roley had some kind of nerve. But I liked the plan. It was simple, and nobody would get hurt.

Theoretically.

32

JAMESON

"Well if it isn't Mrs. Everett."

My mom smiled up at me. "Thank you for calling me that in front of all the school people. It sets a good example."

She'd only drilled it into me all my life. Growing up with a schoolteacher will do that.

Mom beamed as she looked over the festive multi-purpose room, decorated with tissue paper flowers, and whatever else the sixth grade class had decided was appropriate for the Flood Creek School's annual fundraiser.

"Oh my," Mom said, "Mrs. Phelps is not letting some of our guests in." She rushed off.

Old Mrs. Phelps. The stories about her were

becoming more outrageous by the day. And yet they kept her around. It was an incredible act of kindness—one Mom hid from the school board. She was scared to death they'd cut her loose if they knew the school was more adult day care for the old woman than anything else.

"Well. Look who we have here," a voice crooned in my ear.

"Well, shit. If it isn't Melanie Belters. How the hell are you?" It was strange to see her without at least a couple children in tow.

She surveyed the crowd. "I'm tired, Jameson. I tell ya, I'm always fucking tired. Four kids and a grown man who acts like a kid doesn't get me any rest, that's for damn sure. Now if only I can get the cheap bastards here to spend some money tonight, it will be a goddamn miracle. These people send their gazillion children to this school and you think they'd cough up a few bucks for new books or supplies? Hell no. And now we're pushing for a new building before that old piece of shit collapses on everyone. I don't know how we'll fucking pull it off."

"Melanie, you talk to your kids using that language?"

She winked at me. "Every day, baby." And she sauntered away, presumably to shame some parents into opening their wallets.

As far as I knew, she'd always managed to raise the money the school needed and then some. It was hard to say no to that woman.

The event was teeming with the usual suspects, mostly folks I'd grown up with who now were parents, as well as Roman and Cam, whom Ruby had brought. She'd come up with the brilliant idea of creating a weekend getaway package at the ranch to contribute to the silent auction, and there was actually a line at the sign-up sheet.

It was a good sign.

Across the room, I spotted Ruby making the rounds. As a teacher at the school, albeit a temporary one, she really looked in her element. Comfortable and chatty, and of course, freaking beautiful.

She was wearing what she jokingly referred to as her 'New York clothes'—a plain, black, sleeveless dress and high-heeled shoes. No one else in Flood Creek dressed like that, but no one batted an eye in her direction, either. They knew she'd just gotten off the bus from New York, and many still regarded her as a somewhat exotic creature.

And it turned out, I wasn't the only person admiring our lovely girl.

Our girl.

Down boy.

The jerk I'd roughed up at the bar a few days before, Dale, was waiting for Ruby to finish with the mayor so he could pounce on her. Some guys just never learned their fucking lesson. So, while he kept his eye on Ruby, I kept my eye on him.

"Jesus, look at all the people signing up for a weekend at the ranch," Cam said, sipping the disgusting pink punch. "Who knew so many people wanted to spend time at our place."

Roman joined us. "They know it's the nicest ranch around, and Ruby created an awesome package. They get to stay in one of the new bunkhouses and have their meals with us in the main house. And you know Mary can put on a spread. They get free run of the ranch, the pool, everything."

Shit. A lot of people would like a vacation like that. Starting with my mother. And now the wheels were turning.

"You know guys, somewhere down the road we could offer stuff beyond ranch activities, like massage and all that spa kind of shit that people eat up."

Roman slung an arm around my shoulder. "I knew I had you around for a reason, Jameson. Keep coming up with those ideas."

Cam laughed. "Yeah, man. We'll just get that little permitting issue taken care of, and we'll be on our way."

Small detail. But I felt optimistic. Like it was all within reach.

Unfortunately, when I turned around, I found Ruby was within Dale's reach, where he was hovering over her with his cheesy-ass smile. She was trying to be polite, backing away discreetly, but glancing around the room in a panic.

"Oh boy," I said to the guys, "looks like Dale's got his hooks in Ruby again."

Roman squinted across the room. "Is that the jerk you roughed up the other day?"

I nodded.

Cam set his beer down. "I think it's time for the three of us to have a little talk with him."

"Oh boy," Roman said.

We crossed the room and positioned ourselves right behind him.

"Hi, Dale," I said.

He glanced over his shoulder, for some reason thinking he could ignore me.

That was his first mistake.

So I tapped him on his shoulder.

"Dude, I'm busy," he snapped.

I looked at Cam, who rolled his eyes, and Roman, who smirked.

It wasn't that I enjoyed being violent. But when it involved Ruby, there wasn't much margin for error. Assholes were either going to back off or pay the consequences.

Like Dale was about to.

I reached for his shoulder and whipped him around. Ruby's eyes widened, and she stepped back several feet.

Dale's eyes, on the other hand, narrowed and grew dark when he saw I was the one interrupting.

"Hey, loser," he said, "didn't I tell you I was busy?" He puffed up his chest, but when he saw Cam and Roman with me, faltered a little.

Smart man.

I got in his face. "How many times do I need to tell you to leave Ruby alone? Seriously, Dale. How stupid are you?"

He looked from one of us guys to the other, his lips

pressed tightly together. "Fine. You can have the bitch. She's nothing special anyway. She's fucking twenty-eight years old and still single. Good luck with that."

Ruby's mouth dropped open and she took a step toward him just as he started to walk away. As he did, Ruby booted him sharply in the ass. He fell to his knees, attracting the attention of others at the fundraiser. People looked for a moment, then turned back to what they'd been doing.

A minor scuffle like ours was of little interest to anybody else. We were in fucking Montana, after all.

"ANYBODY WANT to join me for a drink?"

Ruby looked at us wickedly as soon as we returned home, and headed for the great room, glancing back over her shoulder and beckoning us with her finger.

Well shit. I wasn't an idiot.

And neither were Cam or Roman.

We took seats on the oversized leather sofa and chairs and Ruby served us scotch after she turned on some soft music.

"What are you drinking, darlin'?" Cam asked, sitting with his arms spread over the sofa back, smiling from ear to ear.

"Nothing yet," she said, reaching to unzip her dress while she moved her hips to the music.

"You sure Mary's gone home?"

She nodded. "Already checked."

She let one shoulder of the dress fall forward and then the other. She turned around, her back to us, and let the dress glide down her hips to the floor. There she stood in a lacy black thong, bra, and high heels, showing off her round little ass.

I shifted in my chair, my dick aching from a hard-on. Out of the corner of my eye I saw the other guys doing the same.

She had that kind of effect on us.

Ruby leaned down to remove her heels, but Roman stopped her. "Keep 'em on, honey."

With her back still to us, she looked over her shoulder and smiled. "Whatever you say, *Mr. Maxwell.*"

Roman's eyes grew wide.

That's what I'm talking about.

She waltzed over and stood before him, slowly removing her bra.

"Give me your tits, baby," he growled.

Ruby obeyed by cupping her breasts and presenting them to him like a gift. He put his hands on her thighs and pulled her until she straddled his lap. Moving her hands, he replaced them with his own, pulling her nipples into his mouth, switching back and forth between the two.

As she arched into his mouth, her head dropped back. Moaning, she ground against him.

Coming up behind her, Cam pushed aside the thin fabric of her thong panty and ran his fingers through her slit, first making circles on her clit, and then finding their way inside her. She pushed her ass back toward him for more and he ran his hand over the erection straining the fly of his blue jeans.

Not one to be left out, I moved toward the three of them and put Ruby's free hand on my dick. She looked at me and smiled, helping to open my pants so she could get her hand on me. She stroked up and down my shaft and I bent to kiss her, driving through her grip as I fucked her hand. Then, she leaned in my direction and took me in her mouth, all the way back to her throat.

"Such a wet pussy. I think you should fuck her right there, man," Cam said, passing Roman a condom.

Smiling, he pulled his cock out of his pants and sheathed himself. Ruby slipped aside the thong, and hovered over Roman while she continued to suck my dick.

Fucking A. She was incredible.

Roman gripped her ass, spreading her cheeks for Cam's viewing pleasure, lowering her until she moaned through her mouthful of my dick.

Tits bouncing, she pistoned on Roman. He furiously fucked her up and down while she twisted in my direction to continue sucking my cock. I knew it wouldn't be long before I blew my load, and I wanted to make it last as long as I could.

But sometimes, a guy just can't.

Cam put a finger in his mouth and even though I couldn't see from my angle, I knew where he was going with it. He circled it around her behind, and I knew he was working his way in when she responded by sucking me even harder.

With one more drive into her mouth, I let loose my load, pulling out when I was only half done to watch my cum spurt over her pretty lips. She shuddered and her eyes fell closed, and I realized Cam had penetrated her ass while Roman continued to fuck her pussy.

As her orgasm erupted, she tossed her head around, her hair flying around her face and whipping Roman in his. Her nipples puckered and her mouth fell open as she screamed for the release we'd so mercilessly led her to.

Roman's head dropped back on the sofa and he growled. "Fuck baby, I'm coming. Squeeze my cock, baby, squeeze it with your pussy."

He bellowed as he pulled Ruby down on his dick one more time. She squealed and shuddered through another orgasm.

Holy.

Fucking.

Shit.

33

RUBY

I PULLED A BLANKET TIGHTER AROUND ME AGAINST THE great room's night chill, lying across Cam and draping my feet over Jameson. Roman sat on the floor in front of me, leaning against the sofa, where I stroked his head with my fingernails.

Holy shit. I was surrounded by three gorgeous, sexy men, who—*by the way*—all liked me.

Me!

I snuggled into Cam's lap and he responded by deliciously twirling my hair. I was a sticky mess, covered in semen and the juices of my own excitement. I was sore— my ass, my pussy, and even my jaw from sucking so much cock. And I'd never felt better.

Before I went to bed that night—or would it be in the

morning?—I planned to take a nice, long bubble bath, maybe with a lit candle or two.

"Hey, Ruby, you were talking to Mayor Burke for a while tonight at the fundraiser," Jameson said.

"Oh my gosh, in all the excitement, I almost forgot to tell you guys."

"What?"

"So, I got to talking to the mayor, and I asked if he was going to bid on the ranch weekend I put together for the silent auction. He said his wife Tilda already had, and in fact, she kept going back to make sure she wasn't outbid."

Jameson groaned, and I lifted my head to look at him. "What?"

"She's a gossipy pain in the ass. That's all. Keep going."

"So, I was telling him that I really hoped he and Mrs. Burke won it, because then they'd be able to see firsthand what a lovely place it is to visit."

The room was dead silent except for the grandfather clock my parents had left behind.

"I told him that regardless, he and the missus should come by sometime and I'd show them around. We could sit by the pool, have a nice lunch, go for a ride, whatever they felt like. Of course, he said that sounded lovely."

Which was when I knew I was reeling the man in. Sometimes you just needed a woman to take care of business.

"Because I had his attention, I told him how great it would be when the ranch was built out and accepting guests. That it would put Flood Creek on the map, be great for the economy with all the people who would be hired, and all the taxes that would be collected. I also pointed out that not only would we have guest accommodations, but also meeting and event spaces, like for conferences and weddings and so forth."

I had to stop and catch my breath, I'd been babbling so fast.

Roman reached for my hand on his head and brought it to his lips. "Sweetie, I'm not sure you should have taken it upon yourself to lobby the mayor on our behalf."

"Yeah, Ruby. We appreciate it and all, but it's a complicated matter. It could have worked against us."

I'd anticipated the guys' being uncomfortable with my initiative. But that was okay, because I was prepared to address their concerns.

Shit, I almost felt like I was back in New York, at work.

Pushing off Cam and Jameson, I popped to my feet, wrapping the blanket around me like a cape.

I raised a finger. "I thought about that. I thought about everything you've just said. And I want to say that is exactly *why* you need me to get involved. I am a fresh pair of eyes on this problem. That, coupled with my marketing experience, means that I can approach the issue of getting the town on board in a different way. I don't have the baggage or history with this that you guys do. I was able to chat with the mayor in a way that none of you guys probably could have."

I watched them consider my words. They slowly

nodded, and their approval turned into appreciative smiles.

Bingo.

"I gotta tell you guys," I said breathlessly, "he was totally receptive. And I'm not exaggerating. I shared with him how during my time in New York, people were super curious about ranch life, and were all dying to experience it. We could get people here from all over the world."

Jameson held his arms open. "Come here, you little mover and shaker."

I ran and jumped into his lap, and the guys high-fived each other.

IT WAS with a spring in my step that I headed to school the next morning, ready to tackle anything that might come my way—misbehaving children, spilled paint, and even dirty looks from Mrs. Phelps—nothing could bother me.

Until I saw Roley on the front steps of the school.

I hadn't told any of the guys he'd called me a whore. Initially, I was so shocked it didn't even occur to me. I just wrote him off as a crank. But after some time, I realized they needed to know. The question was, when to tell them? They were protective—I'd seen how they reacted to Dale—and they'd be pissed. Actually, they'd be furious. Roley would be out of a job. I wasn't sure I wanted to give life to that sort of drama.

I'd tell them eventually. I just had to pick the right time.

I skipped up the school steps with my gaze fixed on the door, intending to walk past Roley and completely ignore him.

But he stepped in front of me, blocking my way.

There was no one else around.

"What do you want?" I hissed. "I thought you didn't talk to whores," I taunted.

Immature? Yes.

I didn't care.

His eyes grew hard and he took a step toward me. He hadn't been so aggressive the other day. It threw me off.

The smell of his unbrushed teeth made me want to vomit.

"A whore like you doesn't belong in this town."

For a second, I was speechless. He really was crazy.

Then, fury rose in me. I pushed past his skinny form, shoulder chucking him hard. "Go to hell, creep."

He called after me as I ran up the steps. "If you don't leave town, Ruby Lee, I'll tell everyone what goes on at Flood Creek Ranch. You'll all be ruined. *Ruined*. Leave town, Ruby Lee, I'm warning you—"

I wanted to scream *fuck off*, but didn't dare to on school premises.

The moment I was inside, I yanked the door shut behind me and leaned against the wall, not sure whether I was going to pass out, throw up, or both.

I was going to kill that little weasel. Actually, I wouldn't have to kill him. One of the guys surely would.

But what if it was too late? What if he'd already told people that I was messing around with the guys?

That they were essentially 'sharing' me?

Fuck, fuck, fuckity fuck.

I was in a near panic state when Mrs. Everett came rushing down the hall toward me. I took a deep breath and put on my best fake-smile.

"Honey, you look a little pale. You feeling okay?" she asked, touching my forehead. "Or did you drink a little too much last night at the fundraiser? Wasn't that fun?"

She continued babbling about how they were well on their way raising funds for a new school building while I tried to figure out what to say. I needed to get out of the school and out of town. I couldn't bring the guys down. They had so much at stake—their investment, their future, their reputations.

I should have just stayed in freaking New York City. At least there, I wouldn't be a threat to anyone's livelihood. Except my own.

"The reason I was looking for you, Ruby, was to tell you that your temp job here might turn into something permanent. So I just wanted to plant that seed. I don't know how long you were planning to stick around Flood Creek, but if I can get permission from the school board to bring you on permanently, I sure hope you'll consider. We love having you around."

Well, not everyone loved having me around.

"That's awesome, Mrs. Everett. I'll give it some thought. For sure."

I excused myself and headed for the teachers' lounge

for some coffee, running smack into the bitchy teacher who'd been making eyes at Cam the week before. What was her name? Missy?

"Morning," I mumbled, doing my best to avoid any more conversation before I got to class.

"Oh, Ruby Lee. Hello."

She sidled up to me, reaching for a sugar for her coffee. When she did, she jostled my arm, spilling half the coffee out of my cup and onto my hand.

"Shit!" I yelled.

She gasped and her eyes opened wide. "Ruby Lee, we don't talk like that around here."

I wanted to tell her we didn't burn people with coffee either, but I decided to skip it.

"Hey, how is Cam, by the way?" she asked, shimmying her shoulders.

Really? She was going to hit me up for info on Cam after nearly burning the flesh off my hand?

"I don't know. Why don't you ask him?" I snapped.

She shrugged. "I plan to. You know, he and I are quite friendly. It's just a matter of time before he asks me out. I know it. He's just shy. It takes guys like that a while."

He sure as shit wasn't shy the night before, but I didn't share that tidbit with her.

Not that any of that mattered. With Roley up my ass, I knew what my next move had to be. I wasn't happy about it, but for the first time since I'd arrived, I knew what I had to do. And it started with packing my bags.

34

CAM

"Well, look who it is."

Ruby glanced up at me with a blank look as if, for a moment, she didn't recognize me.

"Somebody's lost in thought."

I could swear she grimaced for a moment and forced a smile. But I knew her well enough to recognize that something was going on.

The question was, would she tell me?

"Cam," she finally said, touching my forearm in greeting. "Just taking a little walk during my break between classes. I needed to clear my head."

I didn't like the way her shoulders were slumped. "Do you have time for coffee?" I asked.

She looked around for a moment. "Yeah. Let's do it."

We settled into the diner after saying hi to most everybody. I had to wonder if those greetings would be any different if Roley spread the information he was threatening to. Montana, and Flood Creek in particular, were places where people were viciously independent. You lived according to your own rules… up to a point.

I wasn't sure where that point started and ended, but if Roley had his way, we'd be finding out.

But I had good news, and I was dying to share it. I leaned forward over the table and lowered my voice. "Ruby, I think your little talk with the mayor the other night loosened things up for us."

Her eyes opened wide and hope flooded her face.

Bingo.

I was all about making our girl happy.

"Our attorney just met with the planning board. We thought it was best to let him handle the meeting, and he tells us things are looking good. The board is getting back to us after a closed door meeting, but he said they didn't have any real objections to our plans."

She clapped her hands. "Do you think the mayor talked to them?"

I shrugged. "He must have. Who knows how these things work?"

I wish I did. Could have saved us all some time and money. And worry.

She looked down at her hands, and that beleaguered look returned to her pretty face. "I'm so glad. For all of you."

I reached for her hand. I didn't care who might see.

"Okay. What the hell is going on? You look like you lost your best friend."

"I don't know how to tell you this. So I'm just going to tell you."

A spike hit my stomach. I didn't like the way she sounded. At all.

"Ruby, what? Tell me what?"

"I'm leaving town. Not sure when, but soon."

Holy shit.

I hadn't given a lot of thought to how long Ruby would stick around. I guess I naively assumed that as long as our relationship grew, the more likely it was that she'd become a permanent part of our lives. I knew Flood Creek didn't have a lot to offer her, but I'd hoped that because of us guys, its appeal might have grown.

"I... I hope you don't mean that."

She nodded sadly. "Roley threatened me. Told me if I don't hit the road, he'll tell everyone in town what we've been doing. You guys have worked so hard and invested so much, I can't risk ruining that for you."

Her selflessness made my heart break a little. She would sacrifice her happiness for us.

But what she didn't know was that we guys would sacrifice *our* happiness for *hers*.

"I don't think you have to do anything that drastic, Ruby. We are aware of the Roley problem. We are taking care of it."

I didn't want to say much more than that. But the plan was in motion.

"What do you mean? He went to you guys too?"

I nodded. "Yup. He's shaking us down."

She put her hands on her face. "Oh my god. I'm so sorry."

"Ruby, this is not your fault. You haven't done a damn thing wrong. The bad is on us. We hired the creep."

And we would get rid of him. Soon.

"You know, Ruby, we all go through shit."

She looked up at me, surprised I was taking the conversation in this direction.

I looked out the diner window at the street, buildings, and people I'd known all my life. There'd been a time when I thought I'd leave. See the world. Challenge myself. But it didn't turn out that way.

"Ruby, I'd wanted to go to college, just like you. But when my girlfriend got pregnant, all that flew out the window."

She nodded.

"I didn't marry her, as everyone knows. But they don't know what had really happened."

She creased her brow. "You said things were complicated. What did you mean by that, if you don't mind my asking?"

It still killed me to talk about this. It was such an excruciating betrayal, especially by the first girl I'd ever loved.

Ruby continued. "I've wondered for years how all that went down, but it was never my place to ask. Maybe it still isn't."

I took a deep breath. I'd never told another soul this story. "The complication came about because… she got pregnant by... one of my friends. And out of stupid loyalty, I let him talk me into keeping it a secret."

Her mouth dropped open, but no sounds came out. It was about how I'd expect her, or anybody, to react.

I stared at a hangnail so I wouldn't have to look at her. "I never told anyone."

She leaned toward me. "Why? Wouldn't it have taken all that pressure off you, you know, to marry her and stuff?"

I laughed ironically. "Yeah. Sure would have."

She tilted her head. "I'm so sorry you went through that, and you were so young. Are you going tell me who the father was? Or are you still keeping that secret?"

I wanted to keep the secret. But I also wanted to come clean with her. Everybody, really.

"Ruby, the father of Velda's baby was *your brother*. Your brother Bud. He begged me not to expose him. Said your dad would flip, and kick him out. Not pay for his college."

Ruby's hand flew to her mouth and her eyes filled with tears. "Bud? The father? My brother was the *father*?"

"Yeah. That's why Velda left town. He wasn't going to stand by her and she was hurt. He left town shortly thereafter, too, I think out of shame. By then, our friendship was over."

That happens when your best friend impregnates your girlfriend.

"She didn't care that it was you left holding the bag? Looking like the bastard boyfriend? What about Bud? He didn't care either?"

Sad but true.

"Neither of them cared how I was affected."

She covered her face with her hands. "Oh my god, my brother is a father, my parents are grandparents, and I'm an aunt. And we never knew. Cam, why are you telling me this now?"

Good question.

"Because I'm done covering for people. Sacrificing myself. If I'd spoken up back then, I might have made it to college. Or not. The money we had saved ended up being used for my mother's illness. So who knows."

I'd let one man almost ruin my life.

I wasn't going to let another. Specifically, Roley.

I walked Ruby back to school, but before I left I took her hands. "Please don't make any decisions yet. I'm confident we guys can take care of the… problem. In fact, we were going to ask you to put together a little marketing plan for the resort that we could share with the planning board."

We hadn't realized that was the one thing we'd been missing that might convince them to see our side.

What could I say? We were all learning.

As soon as I got back to my truck, I texted Roman and Jameson.

time to set the plan in motion. right now

35

RUBY

"Ruby? Oh, Ruby!"

After coffee with Cam, I was rushing down the hall to the art room, when Mrs. Everett called after me.

"Oh, hi there, sorry! Just got back from… my walk."

She hurried to me and when she was close enough to speak with a lowered voice, leaned next to my ear. "Next break you get, could you stop by my office?"

My stomach dropped. But I forced a smile. "Sure, no problem!" I said cheerfully.

I scurried to the art room, which was really not much more than a supply closet, and sank into the chair in the corner. Rumor had it that when the pregnant art teacher was still working, she'd slip in here for the occasional nap. I wouldn't have minded doing that right then.

But in five minutes, I had a class of fourth graders to teach.

I was grateful I'd have something to take my full attention for an hour. My head was swimming.

Why did Mrs. Everett need to see me? Had Roley already gotten to her?

What did Cam have up his sleeve to get rid of him?

And could I really put together a marketing plan that would not only help Flood Creek Ranch, but also do it justice the way it deserved? If you were to ask my former boss, Silvie, I was afraid the answer would be a resounding *no*.

So, basically, I was fucked. I'd backed myself into a corner and I had no idea how to get the hell out.

I'd somehow become the town slut, was about to be fired from the Flood Creek School, and had no idea how to put together a marketing plan to promote a resort. Or anything else, for that matter.

Jesus. And I'd thought things were tough in New York. I guess the lesson learned was that wherever you go, you're still always stuck with yourself.

I piled supplies onto my wheeled cart, and headed down to the fourth grade classroom, trying to keep the wobbly thing straight in spite of its bum wheel.

Maybe some of the money from the fundraiser could buy a new art cart. Not that I'd be around to see any of it.

I turned a corner and almost ran smack into Melanie with her baby attached to her chest like another appendage.

She gasped. "Jesus! You scared me."

"Mel, you scared me too. You could have ended up covered in yellow paint."

She put her hands on her hips. "Hey, I wanted to talk to you, anyway."

Oh shit. Another person wanted to talk to me. Why did I even get out of bed that morning?

"Mel, I'm late to the fourth grade class."

She waved her hand. "Fuck those brats. Let them wait."

Um. Okay.

"Look, I wanted to talk to you about the high school reunion coming up."

Was she kidding?

"What? Now? Why can't that wait?"

She looked like I'd slapped her. "Because it's important. But if you don't see if that way, then fine." She walked past me and headed for the door.

"Melanie, come back. Tell me what's going on."

Victorious, she returned. "I'm putting together the committee. We need you to write a marketing plan."

Where did everyone get the idea I was some sort of marketing whiz? And why did a high school reunion need a freaking marketing plan?

"Melanie, I'm not sure I'll even be here for that."

Her face fell. "Oh. I see."

I wasn't about to spill the multiple dilemmas I was facing right then and there, if for no other reason than I couldn't walk into a classroom with a tear-stained face.

"That's a bummer, Ruby," she continued, "because

from what I've heard, you're doing a great job here. The parents love you."

What? Was she kidding? The parents loved me? They'd actually said that?

"Really?" I squeaked.

She laughed. "Yeah, dummy. Why are you always the last to know everything?" She patted her baby's behind and sashayed down the hall in her velour tracksuit.

MELANIE'S WORDS lifted my spirits long enough to get by in the hour-long class, but we ran out of red paint toward the end. You'd think that with the drama that ensued, arms had been chopped off.

"He got more red paint than I did!"

"I can't finish my paining!"

"The old teacher never ran out of red!"

Made me wish I were a fourth grader again, where the biggest thing I had to worry about was paint in freaking art class.

I had a little break, not long but enough, before my next class so I wheeled my whole cart of shit to Mrs. Everett's office. I didn't even bother taking off my smock, so I could just jump into it with the fifth graders. Hopefully, they wouldn't have a crapload of complaints about no red paint.

I'd lie and tell them it was toxic or something.

Mrs. Phelps looked up from a newspaper when I

ambled through the office with all my things. She sighed loudly and went back to her reading.

"Mrs. Everett?" I asked, knocking on her doorjamb.

You couldn't knock on her door because she had no door. The hinges were still there from god knew how long ago, but whatever had happened to the door was probably lost to the history of the school.

Mrs. Everett waved me in. Looking around, I realized there was no room for my cart, so I left it outside.

It wasn't New York, I reminded myself. I didn't have to constantly worry about people stealing.

"How's it going, sweetie?" she asked, shuffling some papers.

Shit. Should I just get to it and thank her for the opportunity to work at the school for a while? Tell her that her son Jameson was a good man, and that I never should have left him?

And that I knew she knew—along with everyone else in Flood Creek—that I was the town whore, and that I'd get the hell out of Dodge as soon as I could?

"So, what do you say, Ruby?" she asked.

Huh?

"I'm sorry. My mind wandered for a moment. I... um... didn't get much sleep last night."

Shit. Why did I say that?

But she just smiled kindly, like she always did.

"Ruby, we want you to stay on at the school. We just got the req approved. And, you're getting rave reviews. The kids love you, which means the parents love you."

What? Stay at the school? Like in a job?

Bless her, she saw the confusion on my face. She repeated herself. "You seem to like teaching art, Ruby. We'd love for you to continue, if you're interested."

Oh. I'm not getting fired?

"Sorry, honey? Did you just say something about getting fired?" she asked.

Jesus, I was losing it. First, not listening, then mumbling incoherently.

"Sorry. Mind wandering again."

"So what do you say, Ruby?"

I took a deep breath. "Mrs. Everett, I don't think I'm going to be in Flood Creek for much longer. I'm so sorry. I am beyond flattered to be offered the position. I truly am. I never expected anything like this when I came back to town, and you can't imagine what it has meant to me."

She sat back in her chair, twirling a pen. "You're welcome, honey. Instead of saying no outright, why don't you think about it? You know, sleep on it?"

The woman was an angel, plain and simple.

I stood, knowing the fifth grade class was waiting on my almost-fired-but-offered-a-job town-whore ass.

"I will Mrs. Everett. Thank you."

36

ROMAN

"WHAT'S THIS ABOUT YOUR LEAVING TOWN?"

Ruby wandered into my office and sat on the sofa, pulling her feet up under her, and hugging some ugly needlepoint pillow her parents had left behind.

She eyed her nails to avoid looking at me. "I gotta go, Roman. You don't need me here to mess things up for you."

I played along. Briefly. "Can you get your marketing ideas down on paper before you take off?"

Her head snapped back in surprise, most likely because I didn't try to talk her out of leaving. I planned to—just not yet.

After the shock of the initial insult passed, she forced

her face into something resembling cheerfulness. It was pretty unconvincing, with her weary smile and sagging shoulders.

"What a great idea, Roman," she chirped. "I'd love to. I'll work on it tonight. I only hope I can do the place justice."

She looked around the office, which held a lifetime of memories for her. But the place was mine now—well, mine, Jameson's, and Cam's—and we'd be making our own, new memories.

Hopefully with Ruby by our side.

"That'd be so awesome, baby. I know you'll knock it out of the park."

She nodded. "I love this place. I have a lot of ideas and I promise to put my heart into it."

Raising her chin, she stood to leave, turning quickly to hide her quivering bottom lip.

"Darlin'?" I called after her, watching her shapely form head for the door.

"Yes, Roman?"

"Do me a favor. Stop saying you're leaving. You're not going anywhere, for Christ's sake."

"WHERE IS HE?"

"In the barn," Cam said. "And not happy."

Nor should he be.

Roley sat in a chair in the middle of the old barn, the dilapidated one no longer used for much more than storage. It was the perfect place to interrogate our ne'er do well ranch hand without interruption. And as pissed as Roley looked, he wasn't tied up or held at gunpoint. He could get up and leave, or try to, anytime he wanted. But he sat there, not saying a word.

Maybe he was a little smarter than I'd given him credit for. While he wasn't restrained, if he did decide to split before we were done with him, he'd have the three of us to deal with. And *that* wouldn't be pretty, at least not for him.

"Roley," I started, "did the guys tell you your dad is on his way here? He's going to be providing us some materials for our build out. I'm sure you'll be glad to see him."

Alarm washed over his face. He knew something was up, but probably had no idea we'd play hardball the way we were about to. "Huh? My dad's coming to the ranch? He doesn't need to do that. I can take a look around and let him know what you need."

He nodded like he'd be glad to be helpful.

Yeah… no.

I pulled up one of the chairs Jameson had snagged and sat directly across from the scumbag. "Geez. I didn't even think of that. But too late, he's already coming."

"No," he exclaimed. "You can't do that."

"Why?" I asked.

He looked around nervously. "Because. Because it's not a good idea."

I looked at Jameson and Cam. "Are you saying we shouldn't do business with him?"

"Um, no. It's not that."

"What is it then?"

"I… I don't want him over here."

I cuffed him on the shoulder. "Oh, you don't mean that. He's your dad."

Roley looked around then around in a panic. "Look, I don't want him here because he'll see the things from his junkyard I've been keeping here."

Bingo.

"Geez. Really? You have things you're hiding from your father? Would they happen to be things you've stolen from him?"

He scowled. "None of your business. They're just things. At least I'm not a pervert like you and your whore."

Oh, shit. Did he really just go there? Did the asshole have some kind of death wish?

"Roley, we might be perverts, but at least we are not thieves. Especially not thieves who steal from our own fathers. As for Ruby, I have half a mind to slap you silly for saying that. She's got more character in her little finger than you'll ever have in your entire being, with your stealing from your father, and trying to shake down your employer. Meaning us."

Cam took a step closer. "It takes a special kind of idiot to steal from your dad, but an even worse one to think you can fuck with *us.*"

Roley pressed his lips together and looked down.

"We're gonna make a deal with you, okay?" Jameson said. "We gathered all the contraband you took from your dad and had hidden around the ranch, and put it up in that cage up there, in the loft. See?" he said pointing with a flashlight.

Roley followed the beam into the dark recesses of the barn, to find we'd moved his stolen goods and stored them where no one could get to them. Visible, but nice and locked up.

He jumped to his feet. "Fuck you. Those are my things. You can't do that."

Cam shrugged. "We can. And we did."

"Here's how this is going to work. You pack up your shit, leave town, and don't come back. You keep your big fucking mouth shut, and in return, we keep your contraband safe and sound where we can share it with your father, should the need ever arise."

"What?" he asked, confused. "I have to leave?"

Was he really that stupid?

I wanted to smack some sense into him. "Don't let the door hit you on the way out."

Jameson narrowed his eyes. "You open your mouth about anything going on here, we'll not only let your dad know about all the stuff you stole from him, we'll also notify the sheriff. And as far as I know, you could very well end up back in jail, since this is far from your first offense."

Roley pursed his lips, finally realizing he was outmatched. "Fine. I'll pack my shit and get out tonight. But you'll pay for this."

"No, Roley, we won't. But you'll pay when we let your

father know that you've been stealing from right under his nose. I'm tempted to just call him and tell him now, that's how slimy I think you are. But I'll give you twenty-four hours to get out of town. If I hear you're back or anywhere close by, your dad will be the one after your ass."

"THEY LOVED IT. They fucking loved it."

Yes.

Ruby jumped up and down, clapping her hands, then threw her arms around me. I didn't think I'd ever seen her as happy. Or as beautiful.

She'd just presented her marketing plan to the town planning board, and they fucking ate it up. Jesus, I would have gotten something like that done ages ago if I had known it was the magic bullet.

"I loved how you said that with the proceeds from the resort we could eventually help open a volunteer-based visitor center in town."

She nodded excitedly. "They were eating out of our hands when they finally realized how the resort would benefit everyone."

Jameson picked her up and twirled her around. "Thank you darlin'. We couldn't have done it without you."

"Hell, yeah," Cam thundered. "Those old farts not only approved our permits, but two of them want to invest with us."

Ruby laughed as Jameson set her down. "It's incredible. Just think. If I hadn't left New York, you'd still be arguing with those jerks. You guys *owe* me."

She tapped a finger against her cheek and pursed her lips.

Making my dick twitch for about the fiftieth time that day. Which was just an average day of hanging out with Ruby.

And she was right. We owed her and then some.

"What is it you want?" Cam teased, coming up behind her and pressing into her ass.

Jameson ran kisses up her neck. "Yeah, what *do* you want, gorgeous? Because I can think of something to give you. Something you'll like. A lot."

She tilted her head into Jameson's kisses and ground against Cam's cock. Her hand reached for my growing erection, and unzipped my fly.

"I drive a *hard* bargain, guys."

Ugh. Her hand was so fucking nice on my cock. I knew her lips would be on it momentarily and it was all I could do to hold my orgasm. I planned to fuck her into oblivion before I let myself come.

"Did you hear that, boys? Our girl drives a *hard* bargain. The best kind. So, name your price, pretty lady."

I reached inside her blue jeans. I was training her not to wear panties, and she was accommodating me like a champ.

"Well first, I want to be marketing director of the resort."

I flicked her hard clit, and she gulped, her mouth hanging as her eyes flickered closed.

"You'll have to apply. The competition is very stiff," Jameson said reaching under her shirt to pull her nipples.

"Mmmm," she moaned. "I think I can be pretty competitive."

"What's in it for us, should we hire you?" I asked.

"Well, more great marketing ideas. Oh, and I'll stay."

I stepped back. "What? What did you say?"

Cam pumped his fists in the air. "Yeah, baby. What did you just say?"

Her voice broke but she quickly cleared her throat to hide it. That was my girl. She was one tough cookie.

"I'm staying. Here in Flood Creek. With you guys."

"Hot damn," Jameson said, high fiving Cam and me.

"I was hoping you'd say that," I laughed.

She smiled wickedly and squeezed my cock. "You knew I would. You knew all along. Just like I did."

EPILOGUE

"You want me to do what?"

I bit my tongue. My dear friend Posey, in her fancy designer New York riding boots, looked like she was about to have a heart attack.

I held a shovel out to her. "Clean up the horse poop. C'mon. You can do it. It's part of riding horses. You have to take care of them, too."

Scowling at me, she pulled on a pair of gloves. Yanking the shovel away, she scooped a giant pile of horse manure into a can.

I had to run out of the stall before she saw me shaking with laughter. She'd kill me, probably with the very shovel I'd just given her.

I needed a photo. Stat.

I grabbed my phone and leaned back into the stall just as Sunshine let loose a new load on the clean hay Posey had just scattered.

"Goddammit!" she screamed, throwing down the shovel.

Shoveling horse poop might not sound like much of a vacation to some people, but Posey had sworn she wanted the whole ranch experience. And by god, she sure as hell was getting it. I was making sure.

A bunch of my friends from New York were basically our "beta testers." As marketing director for Flood Creek Ranch & Resort, I'd designed an authentic "Ranch Experience" package for guests, along with some other options that involved less horse poop and more sitting around the pool. But Posey had begged for the full experience. Who was I to say no?

I made a note to talk to the guys about the manual labor part of the guest schedule. Were we taking things too far? Making the experience a bit too authentic?

At the end of my friends' stay, I'd get feedback, but I was already thinking the dirty work might have to be scaled back a little. But not entirely.

I had a feeling Posey will have had her fill of ranch life well before the week was over.

It hadn't been easy to get the resort up and running but we'd pulled it off. My marketing plan went a long way with convincing the Planning Board to grant us the permits we needed but it hadn't been a slam-dunk. A couple people opposed the resort because they didn't want Flood Creek to become anything other than what it currently was. But they were eventually overruled when we convinced people that we'd be bringing jobs and money to town. In fact, we offered jobs to the very people who'd protested. They were flabbergasted we'd offered. But we were just trying to show how our expansion was going to benefit everyone.

Roley was long gone, thank god, and his stuff was still squirreled away in the old barn as a sort of collateral against his big mouth. But the truth was, everyone in town, with the exception of Mrs. Phelps and the brand new art teacher, had kind of figured out we four had something going on, even without his spilling the beans.

And nobody gave a shit.

It's funny—small towns can be much more tolerant than most people would ever guess.

As for the guys and me, we were still figuring things out. But we were doing it with a lot of love and laughter.

Which was all we really needed.

Did you like *Her Dirty Ranchers?* Learn about the next
book in the Men at Work series,
Her Dirty Mafia.

I hope you loved reading this book as much as I loved writing it. Please visit my store to learn more about my books, and to buy directly from me!
https://mikalaneshop.com/

ABOUT THE AUTHOR

Dear Reader:

I'm USA TODAY bestselling romance author Mika Lane, and am OBSESSED with bringing you sassy, steamy stories with imperfect heroines and the bad-a*s dudes they bring to their knees. I'll always bring you my signature humor and heat, topped off with a modern-day happily ever after.

My first book ever was *The Day I Ate the Milkyway,* a true fourth-grade masterpiece illustrated with crayons and bound with construction paper and glue. Nowadays, steamy romance gives purpose to my days and nights as I create worlds and characters that tickle the imagination.

I live in magical Northern California with my own handsome alpha dude, sometimes known as Mr. Mika Lane, and two devilish cats named Chuck and Murray.

A dual citizen of the United States and Ireland, I have on more than one occasion spent my last dollar on a plane ticket somewhere, and am always planning my next escape. I often try new recipes on unsuspecting friends, search out hiding places to read undisturbed, and sadly kill every houseplant I bring home.

I LOVE to hear from readers when I'm not dreaming up naughty tales to share. Visit my online shop https://mikalaneshop.com/ and say hello https://mikalaneshop.com/pages/meet-mika.

xoxo, Mika